THE GUARDIANSHIP SERIES
BOOK #1
(Soup for a Dragon)

Passage to Stomio

Rachel Econ

Passage to Stomio

Published by Wheatmark ®

610 East Delano Street, Suite 104, Tucson, Arizona 85705 U.S.A.
www.wheatmark.com

ISBN: 978-1-60494-145-6
LCCN: 2008930716

Contents

Prologue

TIGER STARED AT the grass in front of her. She just had a vision that would change the life of someone she didn't know. Tiger could not help but laugh at the fact that she was about to go on a journey with some complete stranger who may not know what his or her destiny had in store.

"Well," Tiger said, "Best go find this complete stranger now rather than staring at this grass all night."

She suddenly thought, "What if this stranger is a Human? So much has tormented them that this might completely destroy their lives."

Tiger walked to the edge of the field of grass and looked out to see clouds of darkness gathering. She knew very well why this was happening.

She thought, "Humans again. Yet again, great horror is befalling their race."

There went that sympathy that all Zodiacs

had toward Humans. She turned around to see her dragon, Zatern, staring at her with his bright red eyes.

"Are you ready to go, Tiger?" he asked as Tiger started to climb on to his back. "We have far to travel if we are to make it to the town in your vision."

"Yes, I am ready to go, Zatern," said Tiger.

Zatern stared at her. He knew that something was wrong, and he finally asked, "What is wrong? You seem distant."

"I just have a feeling that something bad is going to happen," said Tiger.

1

Set Some Story

THRESI WAS WORKING hard in the stable. Her older brother had been ill for the last three days.

"He did this on purpose," she thought as she finished mucking out the last stall.

She left the stable immediately after she put away the shovel. She turned toward her house. Thresi, a twelve-year-old girl with wild brown hair and deep blue eyes, was the youngest in her family. She had a fifteen-year-old sister named Aleina and a sixteen-year-old brother named Milo. Her father, Will, owned the only stable in the town of Trenton. Sadly her mother, Anatopa, died not too long ago.

As she opened the door to her house, Milo yelled, "Thresi, could you get me some soup?"

Thresi moaned and yelled, "Yes, your royal painess!"

When she finished making the soup, she

walked to Milo's room and said, "Here is your soup, Milo. Where is Aleina?"

She put down the wooden bowl filled with soup in front of him.

"She's on another date with Otto," said Milo. "What does she see in him? He is…like… weird," replied Milo, taking a sip of his soup.

"My goodness, Milo, you must be sick," replied Thresi.

"Why is that?" asked Milo.

"Well, you just sounded like a girl," said Thresi.

Milo dropped the spoon he was using to sip his soup. He took a moment to recall what he had just said.

"Whoa, you're right, I need to rest for a bit. Could you do me a favor, Thresi?" he asked.

"Sure," she replied. "What is the favor?"

She picked up the fallen spoon, wiped it on her dress, and handed it to Milo.

He said, "Could you go and get Aleina's courting dress? I was going to pick it up, but if I sound like a girl, I need rest."

"She has been courting a lot since mother died," said Thresi.

"Father has pushed her," said Milo. "Even though she loves Otto, she needs to marry someone rich to try and support the family. Now go and get that dress."

She left her brother and headed down into town. Trenton was one of the smallest towns in the country of Quint. Right now, it was quite busy because of a large party that the king and queen were throwing nearby.

While Thresi was walking down the street, she suddenly heard a sneeze coming from a nearby bush. Thresi walked toward the bush to investigate.

"What could have sneezed?" she thought as she peered into the bush.

Inside was a beautiful baby dragon with green skin and dark brown eyes.

The dragon stared at Thresi with its dark brown eyes and asked in small voice, "Who are you? And can you help me? I am looking for someone."

Thresi stared at the dragon with disbelief. Dragons had not been seen in Quint for 200 years.

Thresi replied, "My name is Thresi, and—"

Before she could finish her sentence, the dragon piped up and said excitedly, "I'm looking for you!" the dragon was bouncing around in the bush and let out small, little puffs of smoke from its nose.

"Settle down, little one," said Thresi. "Now what is your name?"

She picked up the dragon and sat down at the side of the road. Thresi started stroking the dragon's small body. The scales felt smooth and cool against Thresi's hand. The stroking seemed to calm the excited dragon, who let out a soft growl of enjoyment.

"I don't have a name," replied the dragon. "You have to name me. Like all the Guardians name their dragons." The baby dragon snuggled into Thresi's arms more.

"Well, I can name you, but I don't know if you are a boy or girl," Thresi said as she rubbed the dragon's head.

"Curious," Thresi thought. "This little dragon is looking for me. But why?"

"I'm a girl, silly," replied the little dragon with a hint of humor in her little voice.

"Because you're a girl, I will name you... uh...Sparks. That's it! Sparks!" said Thresi. Still holding the dragon, she stood up and started walking toward the town. She still needed to get that dress for her sister.

"Sparks, can you go under my dress so we don't attract attention?" Thresi asked.

She knew if she walked into town with a dragon, bad things might happen to her and the newly found Sparks. There were so many guards in Trenton that nothing went unseen. But, if Sparks was under her dress, Thresi would only look fat, which wasn't out of the ordinary.

"Why would we attract attention? Surely there are other dragons and Guardians in your town," said Sparks, starting to climbing down into Thresi's dress.

"Dragons haven't been seen in Quint for 200 years," Thresi explained.

When Sparks found a good spot under her dress, Thresi used her left arm to hold Sparks in place.

Under the dark purple fabric, Thresi heard Sparks say in a muffled voice, "What?"

Thresi walked into the tailor's shop. Nera, the tailor's dog, greeted her. Thresi was petting the dog when the tailor came out.

"Hello, Thresi," the tailor said, smiling. "How can I help you on this fine day?"

"Hello, Stint," said Thresi. "I'm here to pick up Aleina's courting dress." She made sure that Sparks hadn't fallen out of her dress. She was still there.

"Thank goodness," she thought.

Stint went and got the dress from the back of the store. A little while later, Stint arrived with the dress folded in his hands.

"Here you go, Thresi," said Stint, handing the dress to Thresi. "It took quite a while to clean."

"Thank you, Stint. Have a nice day!" Thresi yelled as she left the store.

As Thresi walked down the street, she heard a scream of joy. She followed the sound to an alleyway. Sparks poked her head out from Thresi's dress in curiosity.

As Thresi walked down the street, she heard a familiar squeal of joy. She followed the sound to an alleyway. Sparks poked her head out from inside Thresi's dress in curiosity.

In the alley stood her sister, Aleina, with Otto. They seemed to be flirting, but just as they were about to kiss, Otto took a red knife and stabbed Aleina in the chest. Aleina cried out in shocked anguish as her limp body fell to the dark, cold cobblestones. A low, evil laugh came from Otto as his green eyes turned a dark, almost blood red. He bent over, pulled the knife out, and licked the blade. In horror, Sparks ducked back inside the folds of Thresi's dress. Thresi screamed. Otto turned toward Thresi, but he just smirked and kept licking the blood-soaked blade. Thresi ran as fast as she could back to her house.

She thought, "Why would Otto kill Aleina? Why?"

Tears brimmed in her eyes. She heard the muffled cries of Sparks as she ran toward her home.

2

Add a Man

When Thresi burst through the door of her house, Milo was sitting at the table writing a letter. The force of the door being slammed open knocked over his inkpot. Thresi could feel the distress on her face, and she was sure Milo saw it as well.

"What happened?" Milo asked in a worried tone.

Thresi stared at him, trying to stop crying. She could barely get words out between her sobs, but she managed to say, "Aleina is dead."

Thresi was going to keep how she died to herself. She didn't understand why Otto killed Aleina

"Otto is obviously not Human," thought Thresi.

She got a bowl of the leftover soup.

Milo just stared at her, awestruck.

"She's hiding something," Milo thought. "But what?"

He picked up the fallen inkpot and asked, "How did she die, Thresi? I know you know. And what's in your dress?" Milo used a harsh tone.

Thresi stared at him in awe. The sound of Milo's voice sent shivers down Thresi's spine. With her best matter-of-fact tone, she said, "You're wrong. I don't know how she died. I just saw her body in an alleyway. As for what's under my dress, that's none of your business."

She picked up her bowl of soup and exited the house. She walked toward the forest. When she found a place far enough away, she sat down.

"Sparks, you can come out now," Thresi said.

Sparks peeked her head out of Thresi's collar. In a matter of seconds, her whole body was out of the dress.

"Why didn't you tell your brother about me? Would he hate me?" Sparks asked.

Then she thought to herself, "Why would he hate me? I mean…I'm adorable."

"He wouldn't hate you, Sparks. And you are adorable," Thresi replied. "Wait! I just heard your thoughts!"

Thresi was astonished. Not only had a dragon been looking for her, it could talk and read her thoughts!

"What an odd day," Thresi thought, while petting Sparks.

Sparks let out a growl of enjoyment, which,

sadly, the sound of her hungry baby dragon stomach interrupted.

"Thresi, I'm hungry. Can I have something to eat?" Sparks asked.

Thresi took out the bowl of soup and set it on the grassy ground. Sparks immediately started eating the soup. Ten minutes later, Sparks had licked the bowl clean. Thresi weaved a small basket out of twigs while she waited for Sparks to finish eating.

"Thresi, can I go flying?" asked Sparks when she stopped licking the bowl.

"Of course you can," Thresi said, surprised the little dragon could fly. "Why would you need to ask?"

"I have a strange feeling in my stomach," replied Sparks.

"While you fly, I'll go back to the house to get some food and some of my belongings so we can leave Trenton," said Thresi.

"Why do we have to leave Trenton? I like it here," said Sparks

"It's not safe here. You'll soon probably become too big, and it's hard to hide a giant dragon," replied Thresi. "I'll see you in a little bit."

Sparks flew over the town of Trenton, enjoying the wind as it caressed her smooth, green scales.

"It's wonderful up here," she thought, doing a spin in the air.

Sparks felt her wings grow and stretch. Fire burned deep in her stomach. It left suddenly as soon as it came, and she felt strangly cold. To her, it seemed that all the fire in her body left her. Feeling confused she headed back to the small field she had just left.

Thresi slowly opened the door to her house. She was half-expecting to see Milo or her father sitting at the table, but, luckily, they were in another part of the house. Thresi went to the pantry and put as much food as she could stash in the pack she had brought with her. When she had as much food as she could handle, she started to head toward her room.

Thresi overheard Milo talking to her father in her father's study about Aleina's death and Thresi hiding something under her dress. She figured it was definitely a good thing she didn't tell Milo about Sparks. Milo was such a blabbermouth. She entered her room and collected some of her favorite things which included a pouch filled with dried rose petals that she had gotten at her mother's funeral, a book about weaponry and fighting styles, a pair of leather armbands, and her most prized possession: a book titled, *The Mysteries in our World*. She was heading to the front door when something seemed to call to her. She turned to see her mother's old room. She was never allowed in there. Her father said that her mother's spirit had cursed it. Because she was going to leave, she thought she might as well end her curiosity.

She entered slowly so her brother and father would not hear. She reached the table that was in the center of the room. On the table lay a beautifully crafted, emerald dagger. Thresi picked it up and examined it. She then took it and put it among her belongings. She gave a silent thanks to her mom and left the room.

As she walked by the room where her brother and father were, she whispered, "Good-bye, Father. I hope life will be simpler without me. Milo, I wish you could come, but Father needs you."

After her solemn good-bye, she left her house to find Sparks.

When Thresi arrived back at the grassy field, she noticed that some of the trees were knocked over.

"Strange," she thought. "What happened to the trees?"

Suddenly a sense of burning came over her. She fell to her knees and clutched her stomach. She started to feel as if she was on fire. It was building in her stomach and it pushed on her organs as if trying to find its way out. Soon the feeling mellowed and became a warm spot in her stomach. Thresi stood and continued to walk.

When she got to the middle of the field, she saw a giant dragon. She knew it was Sparks from its coloring, but her wings were now bony with a curved talon at the top of the joints. She looked at her new neck. What was smooth was now marked with jagged spikes laced with a thin skin connecting them and continued all the way down to her tail that now had series of long spikes at the end. Sparks turned toward her.

Thresi stared at the baby dragon's new head. Where Sparks just had little nubs were replaced with spiraling horns that reminded Thresi of a ram.

The dragon said, "Thresi, it's me. Sparks."

Sparks' new voice was deep and sounded as if she was far away.

Thresi stared at Sparks with awe and asked, "How did you grow so much?"

"The soup made me grow. It was chicken noodle," said Sparks. Thresi raised her eyebrow.

"How does that work?"

Sparks shrugged.

"Chicken has special properties. It's a natural way to make dragons grow."

Thresi laughed and said, "That's something I would've never guessed. It's definitely going to be a challenge hiding you now."

Sparks nodded her head.

Before Thresi could climb onto Sparks, she heard a sound coming from a bush. Thresi and Sparks turned their attention toward it. A tall boy with copper hair that covered his green eyes tumbled out.

3

Make Sure the Man Isn't Crazy

The boy landed on his face. Then a black dragon with blue eyes stuck out its head from the trees. It let out a sigh of relief as its whole body emerged from the dense forest.

"Atlas, you klutz! How could you trip on nothing?" the dragon said, picking up the boy with his mouth.

Atlas stared at his dragon and said, "I didn't trip on nothing. I tripped on a bush, which is something."

"A bush is a bush, which is something. Something is nothing, which means you tripped on nothing," replied the dragon.

"Katan, I think you got the lecture I gave you on nothingness confused," Atlas said with a hint of annoyance in his voice.

"No, I think you lectured wrong," replied Katan with pride.

Their argument kept going. Thresi and Sparks just stared at each other.

"I think these two are crazy, Sparks. I really do," Thresi said.

Sparks nodded her head in agreement and then said, "Maybe they are."

They watched Atlas and Katan argue. Thresi noticed that, every time Atlas said something, she could see that he had sharp teeth. They looked like they were meant to rip flesh off meat or bones. It reminded her of her mother's teeth.

Her mom always refused to eat vegetables. She'd always say, "Vegetables are Zodiac food."

Thresi never understood what her mother meant, but it made her laugh.

Sparks went toward Atlas and Katan. Both were still arguing about nothing being something or something being nothing. It was things that were strange to talk about and made no sense. She growled to get their attention, but it didn't work.

She yelled, "Would you two shut up!"

That really got their attention. Thresi took out her mom's dagger and unsheathed it. She walked toward Atlas.

As tough as she could, she asked, "Who are you? Why are you here?" Thresi raised the dagger toward Atlas.

Atlas let out a laugh and that made Thresi angry because he didn't take her seriously.

"Girl, are you really threatening me with a dagger?" he asked. "Have you not heard the saying, 'Never bring a knife to a sword fight'?"

He patted the sword that was attached to

his belt. He smiled and showed his sharp teeth. Thresi glared at him.

"As to who I am and why I am here, listen closely," he said. "I am Atlas of the Dorande Clan. I am here to find and help a girl named Thresi."

Thresi just stared at him. Sparks growled and went behind Thresi.

Thresi put away her dagger and said, "That's me."

"You look to be thirteen, so you must be who you are," Atlas said.

He was still smiling, which made Thresi smile. She took the moment to look him over. He was around six feet tall with a strong, muscular build. His long, copper hair partially covered his face. She turned her attention to his eyes. They were green with a little tint of yellow. She noticed a small tattoo around his left eye. It made him look like he was bleeding.

"He's definitely not a Human," Thresi thought.

"Who is your dragon?" Thresi asked, trying to be as formal as possible.

"Yes," said Sparks, eyeing Katan. "Who is your dragon?"

"My dragon is—"

But Atlas couldn't finish because Katan jumped in front of him and said, "I am Katan." Katan walked toward Sparks. "Who are you? Thresi's dragon?"

"I am Sparks, who else would I be?" Sparks replied.

"A Pretty one that's who," Katan said with a silly grin.

In an awkward silence, Thresi and Atlas just stared at the two dragons.

Thresi finally said, "Atlas, you look a lot like my mom."

"That's because your mother was my older sister," said Atlas.

4

Sprinkle Some Background

THRESI GAZED AT him with a blank stare. Atlas kept smiling at her.

"That's impossible. My mother was Human…I think," Thresi stated.

She scowled at Atlas, who laughed. But Thresi still glared at him.

"Thresi, your mother was a Rogue like me. She wasn't Human," replied Atlas, showing his super-sharp teeth.

Thresi looked at him questioningly before responding, "What's a Rogue?"

"You don't know what a Rogue is, but you are part Rogue," said Atlas, distressed. "Did my sister ever tell you that she was a Rogue? Any clues at all?"

"She would say that vegetables were Zodiac food, and she had sharp teeth like you. That's all," Thresi said. She turned to see Sparks and Katan talking amongst themselves. She turned back to Atlas. "You still didn't answer my question. What's a Rogue? What's a Zodiac?"

"Rogues are people who only eat meat and live in the country of Arsine. We are known for having nasty tempers. We keep to ourselves. Both genders are equal. We rarely leave our country, but I have to travel more because of my position."

"Odd people," remarked Thresi. "What is your position?"

"The same as yours. I am a Guardian," said Atlas. "Zodiacs are beyond explainable, but I'll try my best. Zodiacs are born with a name of an animal. From the beginning of their lives, they take certain characteristics of the animal they are named after. They live in the country of Stomio and have incredibly long life spans. They invented the Guardianship, but the Rogues befriend the dragons. As for Humans, they got added to this Guardianship out of fairness. Anyway, Zodiacs are the oldest of the four races. They don't eat meat. They only eat fruit and vegetables. Because you are a Guardian, you need to have enough background on both of these cultures."

"What is a Guardian?" Thresi asked.

She went up to Sparks and started petting her head. She turned to see Atlas mounting Katan.

He turned toward Thresi and asked, "Do you know how to ride Sparks?"

Thresi shook her head and said, "No."

"Then get on behind me," said Atlas. "I see

you are already packed. Good. Sparks, follow us."

Sparks nodded her head and asked, "Where are we heading?"

Atlas responded, "Into the forest. To get away from here and protect you from the queen and king. Hang on, Thresi!"

Katan took off with such force that it nearly made Thresi throw up. They slowly climbed in altitude. Thresi pondered what Atlas had told her.

"Wait," she thought. "Atlas said four races. What is the fourth?"

"Yes," thought Sparks. Who or what is the fourth race?"

"I'll ask him when we land," Thresi thought to Sparks.

Thresi was getting tired, so she put her head on Atlas's back and fell asleep.

5

Add a Bit of Tiger

When Threси woke up, she was on the ground, wrapped in a blanket. She removed the blanket and folded it. She stood up to see Katan making a fire. She rubbed her eyes and saw that it was morning.

She walked toward Katan and asked, “Can you hear Atlas’ thoughts? Sparks can hear mine.”

“I can hear Atlas’s thoughts. Every Guardian and his or her dragon can share thoughts, but no one else can. It is between your dragon and you,” Katan answered quickly, preoccupied with preparing the breakfast of pure meat.

“Atlas wasn’t lying about him only eating meat,” Thresi thought.

Atlas saw she was awake and walked over to her. He said, “Stompina, Thresi.” He threw another piece of wood into the already large fire.

"Uh, stompina to you to, Atlas," Thresi said, unsure.

Atlas laughed, but Thresi felt a little embarrassed.

"You don't know what 'stompina' means, do you?" Atlas asked.

Thresi shook her head and said, "No."

"It means good morning in Roguish," said Atlas.

"Oh, I would have never known," Thresi said. "Yesterday, you said there were four races, but you never mentioned the fourth. Who or what is the fourth?"

Atlas smile turned into a frown. He turned his head the other way and asked, "Besides your mother's death, did anyone else die?"

Tears brimmed in Thresi's eyes. She walked toward Sparks and rubbed Sparks' head.

Still turned away from Atlas, she said, "Some non-Human named Otto killed my fifteen-year-old sister, Aliena. She was dating him."

She turned toward Atlas and saw him shaking his head.

"Your sister suffered in place of you," he said in a dark and sad tone.

"What do you mean? She suffered in my place?" asked Thresi.

"Otto is one of the fourth race," said Atlas.

"Which is?" asked Thresi.

"Vampires," said Atlas. "Though, there aren't many left that still take pleasure in killing."

"Don't they suck blood?" asked Thresi.

"They only do that when they're desperate. They kill their victim and then just wring the blood out of the body," said Atlas. "It's horrifying to watch."

"Why would this Vampire want to kill Aleina?" asked Thresi.

"Because she was old enough to find her dragon," said Atlas. "Luckily, he didn't kill you."

"Will he go after my older brother, Milo?" asked Thresi.

"No," said Atlas. "Otto probably thinks he has finished his job."

"Which is?" asked Thresi.

"To kill the next Human Guardian," said Atlas.

All of a sudden, they heard a deafening roar. Atlas and Thresi looked toward the sky and saw a huge, red dragon in the sky. The dragon let out another deafening roar.

Atlas shook his head, sighed, and muttered, "Tiger and Zatern."

Thresi stared at the huge dragon slowly approaching the ground. When the dragon landed, a tall, skinny girl dismounted and turned around. Thresi gaped at the girl. She had black, striped skin with orange hair, long nails, and feline-like teeth. The girl glanced quickly at Thresi but turned her attention toward Atlas. She looked at Atlas angrily.

Atlas bowed his head and muttered, "Hinosla, Tiger stri Zatern."

The girl still glared at him. She turned toward Thresi and smiled.

"Stonti, shalan truistin, mentso natsal de Tiger," she said, bowing her head.

Thresi stared at her and thought, "What in the world did she just say?"

Sparks looked at the red dragon and said, "Hello. What is your name? My name is Sparks."

"I know who you are," the dragon said in a deep, male voice that showed authority and strength. "My name is Zatern." He bowed his head toward Sparks. He turned toward Katan, and they started talking.

Thresi looked at the girl and asked, "Could you repeat that?"

The girl laughed. It wasn't as contagious as Atlas', but it still it had a scent of sweetness in its tone. When she stopped laughing, she looked, confusedly, toward Thresi.

"I'm assuming you don't know Zodian and any Roguish," she said with a little twinge of distaste in her voice.

"I know that 'stompina' means 'good morning' in Roguish," Thresi replied sheepishly.

Atlas stood up and went toward the girl. He took her hand and led her closer to Thresi.

He turned toward Thresi and said, "Thresi, this is Tiger, one of the Zodiac's Guardians. Don't let her intimidate you. As you Humans say, her bite is worse than her bark. The same goes to you, Sparks. Don't let Zatern intimidate you. They act like they are so grown up, but, in truth, Katan and I are older than them."

Atlas smiled. It was obvious to Thresi that they knew each other to the extent that Atlas could try and get her goat. Tiger looked at Atlas, annoyed. Thresi noticed they were still holding hands.

"I wonder if they are a couple," Thresi thought.

"No," Sparks thought. "I think they are just really good friends."

Thresi agreed with Sparks. Zatern and Katan returned from their talk. Zatern immediately went toward Tiger. He sent Atlas a warning growl. Atlas immediately let go of Tiger's hand.

"Sorry, Zatern," replied Atlas. "We're just friends."

"I know, but you did break the agreement that the Rogue and Zodiac Guardians had about finding young Thresi here," Zatern said, scowling.

Thresi noticed Zatern had an air of authority and strictness. He looked like he could overpower just about anything that could stand in his way. Sparks made her way closer to him. Zatern stared at her blankly. Surprisingly, he nestled closer to her. Sparks had the largest smile that Thresi had ever seen before. Tiger looked at Zatern, confused.

"I am humoring her, Tiger. She's young and naïve. It isn't her fault for perhaps having a crush," Zatern thought toward Tiger.

Tiger's confused look slowly disappeared. She nodded her head and thought, "Nice that you are humoring her. Remember, she'll be your companion. It isn't good that she develops a crush on you. It will take away her attention away from Thresi."

"Atlas said he and Katan are older than you and Zatern," Thresi said, petting Zatern's nose.

"Well," Tiger replied, "yes."

"Now, Atlas," she said, turning toward Atlas, "Thresi must get approval with the Zodiac Guardians in Stomio before she travels to Arsine to get approval with the Rogue Guardians."

"I don't think she should go to Stomio with out some fighting training," said Atlas, patting Katan's shoulder. "She doesn't know how to ride Sparks."

"Hello, I am right here," Thresi said, annoyed.

"Oh, sorry," Atlas replied, smiling. He walked over to her and ruffled her hair. "Thresi, how do you feel about learning to ride Sparks?"

"I don't know," said Thresi. "I'm kind of scared of heights."

"Don't worry," said Tiger kindly. "Atlas, Katan, Zatern, and I will be there. Sparks will never let you fall."

"All right, I will learn on one condition," Thresi said sternly as if nothing could change her mind.

"Name it," said Atlas.

"Tell me what's a Guardian!" Thresi yelled.

6

Stir in a Guardianship

Tiger and Atlas looked at each other and then at Thresi. There was a long period of silence.

Tiger was the first to speak. "This is a long subject that will take a lot of time to explain, so I suggest we relocate and eat."

Thresi just stared at her and thought, "Sparks, I think they are prolonging this conversation."

"Think, Thresi," Sparks replied in thought. "Remember when Atlas thought you knew more about Rogues and your mother, but you actually didn't?"

"Yes, Sparks. What is your point?" Thresi thought.

"They must have assumed that you knew this as well," thought Sparks.

Thresi just nodded her head toward Sparks and then returned her attention toward Tiger and Atlas.

She said, "All right, there is a town not too

far from this very spot. We can go there and get supplies. Then we can travel to the forest on the other side."

"Before we do some town-hopping, I suggest we eat some of this beautiful breakfast that Katan and I prepared this morning," Atlas said.

In a matter of seconds, he and Katan were already headlong into the feast of pure meat. Thresi just stared at them. Tiger closed her eyes in mere disgust.

"Relax, boys," Thresi said, smiling. "The food won't automatically disappear. Though there is a good chance that you'll choke yourselves to death at the rate you two are eating."

"Yes, the way you two eat makes me want to puke," Tiger replied, pulling an apple from her pocket and wiping it on her shirt. "My father said, 'Don't eat like a Rogue or risk having the smell of mouth bile fill your life with misery and woe.'"

Thresi gave her a weird look. Atlas and Katan stopped their quest to eat all the food that the party had to laugh at what the girls had just said.

"You see, Thresi," Atlas said with a matter-of-fact tone, "Tiger's father was a bit of a tightwad, but, luckily, her mother wasn't, so we have a perfectly balanced Zodiac at our disposal."

Tiger stared at him and took a little too harsh of a bite from her apple. Thresi and Sparks went closer to the fire and helped themselves to some of the meat.

Thresi decided it was time for answers, so

she said, "Might as well tell me what a Guardian is now while we have some time on our hands."

"You are right, Thresi. This is something that should be told to you, but I'll let Tiger tell you. When it comes to history, she is far more knowledgeable than I am," Atlas responded nervously.

Tiger shot him a look, took her place next to Thresi, and started the lecture, "A Guardian is a person who is chosen by his or her people to defend their race at all costs. A Guardian doesn't usually learn of his or her position until the age of fifteen. A Guardian usually finds out when a baby dragon's mother sends him or her to find this new Guardian. The new dragon and Guardian begin their training right away. Also, if either dragon or Guardian die, both die."

"Why am I so important? I know there hasn't been a Human Guardian for some time, but my race doesn't need me. We are doing perfectly fine," Thresi said, exhausted. All this was coming too fast on Thresi. It felt as if someone had dropped a huge pile of bricks on her, expecting her to carry it.

"You are important to your race because your monarchy is corrupted," said Tiger.

"How so, Tiger?" asked Thresi in caustic tone. "Being Zodiac, you must know everything about the Human government."

Tiger looked at Thresi sympathetically, but Thresi's tone still left its mark.

"This is just as I have feared," Tiger thought. "Her life is just about to fall into ruins."

Zatern heard these thoughts of his Guardian, but he decided against offering support because it might make the problem worse. Sparks felt bad for Tiger.

"Thresi should have been much nicer to Tiger," Sparks thought.

Hearing Sparks' thoughts only annoyed Thresi more.

"Will I ever not hear Sparks' thoughts?" Thresi thought.

"It's not that your government is bad, Thresi," Atlas said in a soothing tone. "King Strot and Queen Lily are not leading your people. The Vampires' leader, Quess, is. Your king and queen are just figureheads. I'm not an expert in government and history. From what I have been told, to save their people and family, they had to let Quess rule through them or risk having all Humans destroyed and Quint becoming Vampire country."

Thresi felt really bad about snapping at Tiger like she did, so she apologized, "I am so sorry for snapping at you, Tiger. It is just so confusing. I guess I just snapped from all this pressure."

"Remember that you asked to know," Atlas said, smiling.

Thresi shot him a look. She was about to say something, but Tiger said, "I forgive you, Thresi. I sort of expected you to react that way. I would have been surprised if you didn't."

They shook hands and stood up.

"All right, let's pack up and head to the town. Sparks, Katan, Zatern, and I will go to the other side of the town and wait for you guys," Tiger suggested.

Atlas started packing while Thresi got out some money.

"Tiger," she asked while examining a coin, "why won't you come with me and Atlas?"

"Because I'll stick out too much," said Tiger. "All right, I will meet you guys on the other side of town."

Tiger mounted Zatern and took off with the other dragons in tow. Thresi and Atlas headed toward the town in a matter of minutes.

7

Sprinkle Some Lies

THRESI AND ATLAS entered the large town of Stientis. Thresi had completely forgotten the fact that the king, queen, and possibly Quess were having a party within the next few days. Thresi looked around to see over 100 guards standing at the gate of the city.

"Atlas," Thresi said nervously, "look at all the guards. How are we supposed to get by them?"

Atlas looked in the direction Thresi was pointing and gave a small nod. He said calmly, "Don't worry. I'll think of something."

Thresi gave him a look of anguish and asked, "Why don't you tell me your plan?"

Atlas laughed and smiled at her.

"No," Atlas said, still smiling. "When we get inside the town, get anything you like. Tiger would say we have to travel light and not get anything other than the necessities. I have missed tons of holidays and birthdays that I, as your uncle, should have gotten gifts for you. Because I just learned of your existence recently, this is the least I could do."

"Thank you, Atlas," Thresi said, smiling.

"I suggest you get a sword," said Atlas. "In any battle, my sister's concealed dagger might not hold its own."

Thresi gave him a small nod. She didn't want to part with the dagger, but, if it was a concealed weapon, she didn't know she wouldn't use it as it was supposed to be used.

As they got closer to the town, Thresi was growing nervous. Atlas sensed her anxiety. Rogues were extremely good at detecting emotion. They were soon only a few feet away from the guards.

Atlas stopped Thresi and said, "Just relax and follow my lead. Cor-ta ka siewr."

Thresi just nodded her head and took some deep, calming breaths to relax, but, sadly, they weren't working.

"Halt," called the first guard.

"A captain," Thresi thought, noticing his red and gold uniform.

Thresi had great knowledge of Quint's military because of Milo. When he really wanted to join the cavalry, he spent every day studying everything about it. He loved to show their mom, Anatopa, and Thresi. Anatopa would help explain things to Milo and Thresi. Aleina was always like their father, Will, and thought it was improper for Thresi to learn these things.

She brought it up many times with their mother. Anatopa laughed and smiled at Aleina.

"I have no reason to stop Milo from teaching Thresi about the art of war."

Aliena frowned.

"War is not an art, Mother, at least not for a girl."

"My dear you disappoint me greatly," Anatopa said with a frown. "Your sister will amount to great things. And where will you be? Sitting on the lap of an old has been noble as his pet!"

Aleina growled and said, " At least I can support this family when you and father become senile!".

"You Little!" Will touched his wife's arm.

"Calm down, Love, Aleina that is a good point and a marvelous idea," he said giving her a smile. Anatopa immediately stalked off to her room.

Anatopa died when Thresi was nine. Aleina immediately told their father about the lectures about the military that Milo was giving Thresi. Milo was punished. Thresi's instructions were replaced with instructions on how to be a lady. Thresi hated those lessons with Aleina.

She would say, " Aleina, why couldn't you let me learn those things Milo was teaching me?"

Aleina would get angry and rant about how Thresi would never be a proper lady and end up like their mother, married to a stable keeper. Thresi hated Aleina purely because of how she talked about her mother and how she couldn't let her be what she wanted. To make matters worse, after Milo was punished, he never wanted to join the cavalry anymore.

Thresi was brought back to attention when Atlas began to speak. He took a step forward and gave a small, two-finger salute.

"My name is Corwin, and this is my younger sister," Atlas said, gesturing toward Thresi.

Thresi curtsied toward the captain and said politely, "Good day, sir."

"And we," Atlas continued, "are here to visit family."

"Who is the family?" the captain asked.

"Travis the Fat," said Atlas.

"Oh…him. Good luck with that. You may pass," the captain said. "Sir Corwin, I wouldn't let the girl handle the dagger. She might hurt herself."

"I'll keep that in mind," Atlas said, scowling.

Thresi and Atlas walked by the guards and headed into the town, Steintis.

8

Stir in Some Evil

STEINTIS WAS FILLED with the sounds of horses, craft workers, children, and the usual bystander. Thresi had been to Steintis before, so she was used to the hustle and bustle of the large town. Atlas, on the other hand, wasn't used to large towns. The expression of pure amazement was written all over his face.

Thresi showed Atlas the many places to buy food while she took some time to look at some shops. Thresi did find a beautiful, green cloak that matched Sparks' scales. Thresi bought a blanket so Sparks' scales wouldn't rub the skin of her legs when she started to practice riding. Atlas and Thresi met up near a small leather shop. Thresi got some strong boots, and Atlas replaced his own.

Their final stop was a blacksmith's shop. Atlas went in and got a sword for Thresi while she picked out a belt to hold the small sword. After picking out the necessary items for their journey, they headed to the city's exit. Atlas stopped a little bit before the exit.

Thresi was about to ask what was wrong when Atlas shushed her. He led her behind some crates and motioned for her to crouch. Thresi looked through the space between the crates. Otto, a man with red hair and red eyes, and a girl with dark purple hair and red eyes came from out of nowhere.

Otto laughed and said, "Nice try, Atlas, but I know you're here. Go ahead and bring Thresi out here. We know each other."

The girl and other boy laughed. Atlas took Thresi's hand and led her from their hiding place.

"Otto, Trip, and Somari. In what do we owe this nightmare?" Atlas asked in a seemingly strong voice.

But Thresi heard a small crack in his voice. The three strangers laughed.

The girl named Somari said, "We found out that Otto killed the wrong person. So we knew you'd come to the poor unfortunate Guardian's aid when she found her dragon."

Atlas unsheathed his sword and said, "Leave Thresi alone. You have no need for her."

All three laughed again.

"Yes, we do, Atlas," Trip said, smiling evilly. "We are all dreadfully hungry."

"Now wait," Otto said. "Let's not forget that Rogue tastes so much better."

That roused a laugh from the other two. Atlas grew rigid. A sad glare showed in his eye.

"They're Vampires," Thresi thought.

She was about to call for Sparks when Atlas nudged her and slightly shook his head.

"Leave us alone. You have no reason to kill us," Atlas said.

"Yes, we do," Somari said.

The small group of Vampires unsheathed their blood red daggers and charged Atlas. Atlas blocked their stabbing motions easily. Trip stabbed Atlas six times in the arm; Otto got him in the back twice. Thresi watched as blood covered Atlas' clothes. Thresi immediately unsheathed her sword and attacked Somari. Somari took quick jabs at Thresi, but Thresi didn't let them pass the impenetrable barrier that she made with her sword. She disarmed Somari with a swift movement and knocked her to the ground. When Somari hit the dirt, Trip and Otto went to her aid, leaving a bloody Atlas fighting for breath. His sword fell to the ground. He stood up quickly and grabbed his sword. Taking Thresi by her sleeve, he led her away, running. They ran until they reached the forest that held Tiger and the dragons.

9

The Smoke May Make You Sick

Atlas and Thresi ran through the forest quickly. Branches and twigs hit Thresi's face and snapped on impact. Thresi knew that her face was bleeding, but she didn't care. She only knew that she and Atlas had to get away from the three Vampires. Atlas's steps were faulting. His vision became blurry, but he kept going.

"How did they find me? I thought I lost them for good," he thought.

They ran blindly until they heard the sound of a sword being sharpened. Both stumbled into a clearing where the dragons were sleeping and Tiger was sitting on a boulder, sharpening one of her short swords. She didn't hear them enter the clearing.

As loud as he could, Atlas yelled, "Tiger!"

Then he passed out.

"Atlas!" Thresi screamed as Atlas' body hit the dirt.

Tiger's feline senses kicked into gear, and she ran to Atlas' aid. "Thresi," Tiger ordered quickly, "lay out a blanket!"

Thresi ran to the supply bags. Her cloak glided along the grass. She grabbed a blanket and laid it on the ground. Tiger carried Atlas to the blanket. She laid him on his stomach on its woolly surface. Tiger bent down and took off his shirt. Atlas moaned in pain as Tiger moved his left arm. She examined his stab wounds and shook her head. She motioned for Thresi to come forward.

"Thresi, wake up Zatern," ordered Tiger sternly. "Tell him to go find the coleniess herb. Wake up Sparks and Katan. Katan will want to know what happened. Send Sparks to come talk to me."

Tiger turned away from Thresi and went to work to stop the bleeding of his wounds. Tiger muttered in Zodian, but its meaning could not pass her mind. Thresi yet again ran to where the dragons were sleeping. Zatern was already awake. Restless, he stared at Thresi with his red eyes. Thresi gave him his orders. Without hesitation, he ran into the forest. Thresi woke up the other two dragons. Katan was annoyed because he had been woken up, but Sparks was happy to see Thresi. Thresi told them about what had happened in Steintis. Sparks' happiness turned into sadness. Katan's annoyance became anxiety as he rushed to the blanket where Atlas lay unmoving.

"Thresi," Sparks asked worriedly, "are you all right?"

Thresi affectionately rubbed Sparks' large shoulder and said, "I'm fine, Sparks. Just a few scratches."

Almost automatically, she touched her face. She felt the ridges of scars as she ran her fingertips across her skin. Sparks let out a sigh of relief and laid her long neck on the ground.

She said, "Get on."

Thresi looked at Sparks nervously and said, "No."

"I'm not going to fly," said Sparks. "I was just going to walk to the other side of the clearing. I have to talk to Tiger, right?"

Thresi nodded her head and clambered onto Sparks' neck. Except for the occasional bird, their walk was quiet. The clearing was beautiful with its wildlife performing the lovely dances of spring. It was hard to believe someone was suffering within its lush sanctuary.

They arrived within minutes. Like a mother caring for her wounded cub, Tiger was caring for Atlas. Natural instincts never really left a Zodian.

"Thresi, use this blanket to make bandages, but be far enough away so Sparks and I can talk alone," Tiger said anxiously.

Thresi took the blanket, left, and sat on a stump. She started to rip the fabric into thick strips. Thresi looked at Tiger, who was talking to the worried Katan. Katan ran into the forest with great speed. Thresi was lost in work, completely oblivious to the sound of giant wings.

"You do know he will be fine, right?" asked a deep voice.

Thresi turned to see Zatern staring at her with his intelligent eyes.

"Who? Atlas? Yes, I know. What makes you so sure?" Thresi responded in a distant tone.

Zatern walked toward her as best as he could while holding the herb in closed talons.

"Tiger told me to wait with you," said Zatern. "That means Atlas doesn't need this herb immediately."

"So he doesn't need a plant. Do you have any substantial evidence?" asked Thresi.

"The coleniess herb is the strongest healing medicine in the world. Humans call it cat's claw," Zatern said calmly.

"I hope you're right, Zatern. I really do," Thresi whispered.

10

When Sick Takes Guilt

"What is it, Tiger?" Sparks asked worriedly.

She was pacing around Atlas, staring at his face. His pained expression roused every bit of sympathy that Sparks could offer. She nuzzled his left arm. Atlas moaned in pain with the soft contact. Sparks moved her head away in sadness, knowing she had caused pain.

"Everything is fine. He braved a huge battle. He's in the clear, but he didn't come out without wounds," Tiger said sadly.

Sparks nodded her head, but she was curious about what Tiger meant.

"What battle did he get into while on this blanket?" asked Sparks.

"The battle of life and death! The one that causes tons of pain! He was passed out. I used a metaphor," Tiger said, exasperated.

"Oh, I didn't know. What so-called wounds did he receive?" Sparks asked.

"He'll never be able to use his left arm again," Tiger said sorrowfully.

"How did that happen?" Sparks asked, shocked.

"From what Katan has told me, Trip stabbed Atlas through the tendon in his arm," said Tiger. "I examined it, and it's ripped to shreds."

"Is there a possibility that it will be fixed?" Sparks asked with despair.

Sparks looked at Tiger with hopeful eyes. Sparks could see that Tiger was worn-out from taking care of Atlas. Tiger's clothes stuck to her body with sweat. Splotches of blood dotted the sleeves of her tunic as well as her breeches.

"Perhaps Zodian healers could do something when we arrive at Stomio, but don't put your hopes up," Tiger said.

She waved toward Zatern and Thresi, summoning them to come over. She asked, "Sparks, could you tell Thresi for me? I couldn't bring myself to tell her because Atlas is her uncle."

"I'll do so immediately," Sparks replied.

Zatern and Thresi came down from their humble stump. Zatern handed the herb to Tiger; Thresi handed over the bandages.

"How is Atlas doing?" Thresi said, quietly but sadly.

"He's doing well," Tiger said quickly.

Tiger didn't look at Thresi at all. She knew that, if she did, she would tell the truth about Atlas' left arm. Thresi knelt next to Tiger and helped her treat Atlas. With an attentive eye, Thresi watched as Tiger took a leaf of the colneiss herb, rubbed into a paste, and smeared it onto one of Atlas' back wounds. Thresi copied her movements precisely and worked on his arm. Atlas let out a moan of pain as Thresi smeared the paste on his arm.

"He must be in a lot of pain," she thought.

She ignored the moan and went back to her work. There was silence as she and Tiger worked, except for the occasional moan from Atlas if Thresi pushed too hard on the wound. Both bandaged Atlas and stood up. Tiger turned Atlas on his back and laid his arm in a sling. Thresi walked away, looking at the sky. She saw half a moon.

Sparks nudged Thresi's back with so much force that Thresi nearly fell over, but Thresi was pretty strong-footed. It was something she had acquired from riding horses her whole life. She also had strength in her upper body.

"What is it, Sparks?" Thresi asked while affectionately scratching Sparks' scaly cheek.

"It's about Atlas," Sparks replied nervously.

Even Sparks didn't know how to break the news to Thresi. So she decided just to say it. She did so without taking any time to breathe. Thresi originally felt better, but her mood sank into the deep pit of anxiety and despair as waves of guilt crashed on its soft shore. When Sparks finished, Thresi was on the brink of breaking into sobs.

"It's all my fault," Thresi said, holding back her tears.

"No, it isn't," Sparks said soothingly. She hated to see Thresi so upset.

"Yes, it is," said Thresi. "If I would have gotten into the battle sooner, I could have— "

"Could have what, Thresi?" Sparks asked. "Ended up with a dead arm? What use would that be to your people?"

"Regardless of my people, Atlas didn't deserve this punishment, especially because he was trying to protect me," Thresi said sternly.

"Atlas knew what he was doing, Thresi," said Sparks calmly. "And you know that. He would give his life for you. Even though I doubt he planned to get his left arm paralyzed, but it was just another way to protect you." She could see that Thresi was starting to cool down a bit.

"I suppose you're right, Sparks," Thresi said.

Her mood was lifted. She loved Sparks and her outgoing, cheery attitude. Sparks was a better sister than Aliena was. In the short time of knowing the Zodian, she felt that even Tiger was a better sister than Aliena was.

Thresi hugged Sparks' neck, feeling the smooth scales with her hands. Thresi's arms couldn't go all the way around the dragon's neck. Thresi looked to where she last saw Tiger. Tiger had put a blanket over Atlas. She was gently dreaming by his side with Zatern and Katan sleeping nearby. Sparks lay down. Thresi lay down beside her, snuggling into Sparks' warm stomach.

11

You Will Get Better Eventually

TWO DAYS PASSED rather slowly for Thresi. She did try occupying her time by weaving baskets from blades of grass and playing a pipe she got in Stentis. The pipe's original sound was as if a bird was singing, but, over time, that bird was on the brink of dying. Tiger, on the other hand, used her time to take care of Atlas, who was still sleeping, and hunting for more healing herbs. The dragons would play small games and go flying every so often, but they mostly slept. Atlas was improving at a tremendous rate. Rogues are quick healers. They had to be able to live on the unforgiving wasteland that was Arsine. When Tiger was taking a break or out hunting for healing herbs, Thresi would take care of Atlas.

During his sleep, Atlas would squirm about and talk. He'd often have nightmares. Many times in his sleep, he'd try to move his left arm, but it was unmoving. Even during sleep, he'd let out a groan of frustration over the paralyzed limb. Thresi hated seeing Atlas in so much anguish, but there was nothing she could do.

The morning of the third day was filled with warmth from the sun. At the far side of the clearing, Thresi was trying to turn her pipe into a pipe instead of a dying duck.

"Why won't this pipe stop squawking?" Thresi said, frustrated.

She blew a harsh, six-fingered note, which woke the sleeping forms of Sparks and Katan that lay beside her.

"Ugh!" Katan yelled, standing and stretching. "What was that horrible noise?"

"I believe it is classified as a squawk, Katan," Sparks said sarcastically, grooming her talons. "You know the sound a bird makes."

Katan glared at Sparks and said, "A dying bird in this case."

"It's my pipe, you two," Thresi said, trying to hold back her laughter.

To prove herself, she let out another note. Katan let out a groan of annoyance. Sparks and Thresi laughed hysterically. But the rather loud landing of Zatern interrupted their laughter.

"You guys," Zatern said, trying to catch his breath, "it's Atlas. He's awake!"

Sparks gasped. Thresi cupped her hands over mouth in surprise. Katan immediately jumped into the sky and flew toward the other side of the field. Zatern quickly followed.

Sparks turned toward Thresi and said, "We

should start walking before he falls asleep again."

"No, Sparks, Thresi said sternly. "Let's fly."

Sparks was excited while Thresi looked nervous. Sparks bent down so Thresi could get on.

"Don't worry, Thresi. This will be fun. Just hold on," said Sparks.

As soon as Thresi was sitting at the end of Sparks' neck, Sparks leapt into a run. Soon, she gathered enough speed to take off. With a leap of force, Sparks was soaring in the sky. Thresi was slowly getting used to the weightless feeling of flying. She tightened her grip on Sparks' neck spikes. Sparks could tell that Thresi was still a little nervous.

"Thresi," Sparks said through their mind link, "there's a beautiful view from up here. Why don't you look? It will make you feel better."

Thresi glanced down, seeing birds flying below her and the waves of grass blowing in the breeze. She did start to feel better. Just as she was starting to enjoy flying, they landed on the grass. Though it wasn't a graceful landing, it was good enough for Thresi not to fall off. A new problem stood. How would she get down?

"Sparks, how do I get down?" Thresi asked while measuring how long the fall would be from where she sat. She came up with 20.9 feet exactly. Thresi was always very good at math.

"Here," said Sparks, "I'll help you."

Sparks craned her neck so her head was by Thresi's body. She pulled off Thresi and put her on the ground. Thresi brushed off her dress and took off running toward Atlas, who was sitting upright against a tree with Katan, Zatern, and Tiger by his side.

Thresi threw her arms around his neck and said excitedly, "Atlas, you're all right!"

Atlas took his right arm and hugged Thresi back. He could feel drops of water land on his shoulder. They released each other, and Atlas saw Thresi's watery eyes.

"Of course, I'm all right. What did you think? I was going to die?" he said with his usual humorous tone. Thresi just smiled and giggled. "Don't worry. I have a long life to live."

Thresi hugged him again and stood up. She asked, "How is your arm?"

She assumed he already knew it was paralyzed. The mention of the word "arm" earned a shaking head from Katan. In the corner of his eye, Atlas caught Katan shaking his head.

"I think it's okay. It's just throbbing, but, if there is something I should know, I would like to know it," Atlas said, glaring at Katan. "Shouldn't I, Tiger?"

Tiger had a nervous look on her face. She cleared her throat and said, "Well, Atlas—"

Before she could go on, Atlas burst out, "Am I dead? I'm in heaven, aren't I? Wow, it looks a lot like Quint. Is this Quint's heaven? Did you guys die, too?"

Tiger shook her head, and Thresi huffed.

"You numbskull!" Sparks yelled, frustrated.

"You're not dead," Katan said.

"Nor are you in heaven," Zatern finished.

"Really?" Atlas asked. The others nodded their heads. "Good. But really what's wrong?" He smiled, showing all his sharp teeth.

"Well, your left arm is paralyzed. Trip completely ripped apart your tendon. There was nothing I could do," Tiger explained sadly.

Atlas' smile turned into a frown.

Katan nuzzled Atlas and said, "Killts ir hu grentics thses Zodian henuens crvebs yitis lt."

Atlas took notice to this comment, but it was no comfort to him. Katan closed his eyes and put his head down into Atlas' right hand.

"Please tell me that you're kidding," he pleaded in a sad voice.

Atlas knew that, with a paralyzed limb, the people of his clan would not accept him anymore. Rogues believed that an injured person was useless.

"I'm so sorry, Atlas. I understand what this means to you," Tiger said sympathetically.

Thresi felt bad for Atlas. He was taking the news very hard.

"I'm useless. Utterly useless," he muttered under his breath.

Katan nuzzled him. Tiger put a hand on his shoulder.

12

A Teaspoon of Secrets

MILO LEFT SOME flowers on each of the gravestones. One read, "Hear lays Anatopa, a loving wife and mother."

Milo felt a tear roll down his cheek. He missed his mother, and he would do anything to get her back. He turned to the other gravestone that read, "Here lays Aleina, a lovely woman."

"That's about the only thing she was," Milo thought.

He turned and left the graveyard, lost in a torrent of memories. He was so lost in his thoughts that, before he knew it, he walked to the alley where they had found Aleina's body. Out of nowhere, a hand cupped over his mouth and pulled him into the alley. He felt the coarse texture of rope go around his hands, and he was kicked to the ground. Milo was in a daze when another kick hit his stomach. The force took his breath away. He staggered up to be face-to-face with a boy with red eyes and red hair. Milo tried to back away, but the boy grabbed Milo by the front of his shirt, enabling Milo to move.

The boy asked, "Where is your sister going, Milo?"

The boy's tone was filled with hate and anger. Milo was nervous. He was at the complete mercy of this boy.

"Heaven, I think," Milo replied coolly. The boy punched Milo in the stomach.

"Not that sister, you dunce," the boy said, scowling and showing his fangs.

He then unsheathed his blood red dagger and held it at Milo's throat. Milo wasn't just nervous. He was scared to death.

"Your sister! Thresi!" the boy said.

Milo looked at him funny and thought, "Why would he want to know about Thresi?"

"I don't know," Milo whispered.

The boy slashed his dagger through the middle of Milo's shoulder. Milo winced in pain. He could tell that the wound was deep. Milo felt blood flow in a steady stream down his back.

"I'll ask one more time," the boy said, angrily pointing the dagger toward Milo's stomach. "Where is Thresi heading?"

"I don't know," Milo repeated and braced himself for the dagger to stab him.

"Milo, where are you?" asked the voice of Milo's father.

The boy used the hilt of his dagger to hit Milo on his head, sending Milo straight to the ground. The blow felt like a rock. The boy pushed Milo out of the alley. The world was turning dark for

Milo, but, before his eyes closed, he saw his father running toward him. Then darkness filled his vision.

Milo woke up on his bed with only candlelight for illumination. His father was sitting in a chair near the door. Milo felt a dull throbbing in his head. He tried to sit up, but the pain in his shoulder told him otherwise. His father came to his aid and lifted him up. Milo put his back on the wall and rubbed his wrists. They were sore and red. Much of the skin was gone.

"How are you feeling, Milo?" his father asked.

His father wasn't bad-looking. Milo looked at lot like him with dirty blonde hair and strange, silver eyes. Many times in his life, Milo was often asked if he was blind. His eyes sometimes looked as if they held his pupils hostage. Unlike most of the men in Trenton, his father didn't have any facial hair at all. He refused to grow any, but it was more likely that he couldn't.

"I'm fine, Father. Just some pain here and there," Milo replied. "May I have some water?"

"Sure," his father said and left the room. He soon returned with a water skin.

Milo took a long drink before setting it down. "Thanks," he said in a tired voice.

"You're welcome," his father said happily. "Now tell me what happened."

"I was walking back from the cemetery when, from out of nowhere, this boy with red hair and eyes pulled me into the alley—"

"Red hair and eyes?" his father interrupted.

Milo nodded his head.

"Continue."

"And bound my hands. He kept asking me where Thresi was going. He eventually pulled a knife on me and cut my shoulder. When you called me, he knocked me on the head. Then I passed out."

Milo looked at his father, who had a look of what could have been anger or sadness in his eyes. His father paced around the room, muttering words under his breath.

"Milo, my boy, I haven't been completely honest with you or Thresi," his father said, looking down at the ground.

"What do you mean, Father?" Milo asked, confused.

His father moved the stool closer to the bed and sat down. He said, "It's about your heritage and your mother. Tell me, Milo, do you believe in lands outside of Quint?"

Milo took another drink of water before answering, "No, I mean Mother told me stories of places called Arsine and Stomio and the strange people who lived there. I used to believe them, but I soon learned that they didn't exist."

"Son, they do exist. Your mother, may she rest in peace, was from Arsine. She was a Rogue. Not just any Rogue. She was a Guardian."

"You're kidding, right?" Milo said nervously. "What's a Guardian?"

"I'll get to that if you let me continue," his father said sternly. "Now, your mother told me this when we first met. She was from a small clan in Arsine called the Dorande. She was born 130 years ago, only three years after I was born."

Milo's expression changed from surprise to shock. His father noticed his expression and chuckled.

He explained, "We actually met in Stomio when her younger brother was visiting a Zodiac friend of his. I forget his name. I believe he was eighty-five at the time. We were 100 and found out we had a lot in common. After ten years of friendship, we got married. She left her dragon in Arsine so he might have a family. Seven years later, you were born. Then we adopted Aliena—"

"You adopted Aliena? How come you're so old? Where does Thresi fit into this?" Milo interrupted again.

This time, his father softly whacked him on the head and said, "What did I say about interrupting me?"

"Sorry," Milo muttered.

"Yes, Aliena was adopted," said Milo's father. "She was left at our doorstep one day. Thresi was born later. I am so old because I'm an All-Seer and so are you. An All-Seer is someone who can look into the future, but, sadly, not his or her own. Thresi fits into this because she's a Guardian. Thresi must have found her dragon and left to go to Stomio. She's probably with your uncle. I'm telling you this because I know you're planning to go after her."

Milo was about to ask more questions, but Will slapped his head again and said, "No more questions, Milo. You need your rest if you plan to track your sister tomorrow."

Milo reluctantly laid down into the soft, warm sheets and closed his eyes. His father blew out the candle and closed the door as he exited the room. Milo didn't fall asleep for a few hours, trying to understand what he had just heard.

"I must do one thing for certain," Milo thought as he started to lull into sleep. "Find Thresi."

13

Add Some Whole Quest

MILO WOKE UP in the morning and got dressed. As he went to get some breakfast, he noticed his father wasn't in the house. He sat down at the table and ate some porridge alone. An ominous feeling was in the air. His vision suddenly went dark. He saw Thresi standing by a green dragon, who had its head bent down. The dragon was nudging a copper-haired boy who looked extremely sad. To the boy's right, a tiger-looking girl stood with a hand on his shoulder. A red dragon was by her side. A black dragon stood to the left of the boy. The black dragon had placed its head in the boy's lap.

The vision faded away to the deep caverns of Milo's mind. He shook his head and continued to eat his food. When he was done, he left the house, went to the stable, and saw his father leading Milo's favorite horse, Blackheart, who was loaded with food and water. The large stallion let out a long whinny as Milo walked down the path.

"I was wondering when you might come down here," his father said, giving Blackheart's reins to Milo. "Listen to me. That boy who grabbed you yesterday was a Vampire. Remember the legend I told you when you were younger?"

Milo nodded his head.

"Listen to it. Follow it. It will be your only way out. And, most importantly, take care," said his father.

"I will," Milo said.

They embraced each other.

Milo mounted Blackheart and said, "Goodbye, Father."

Milo's father nodded his head toward the road. Milo pulled the hood of his cloak to cover his face as he cantered into the town.

First, he needed to track the last place Thresi might have gone. He slowed Blackheart to a walk and studied the road for clues. Stint's dog, Nera, walked up to Blackheart.

"Hey, girl, can you help me? I'm looking for Thresi," Milo asked the white dog.

Immediately, Nera shot off like lightning into the forest. Milo quickly reined Blackheart after the dog. He ran until they reached a clearing where several trees were knocked down. Nera stopped, sat, and wagged her tail. Milo dismounted and patted the dog on her head. He suddenly remembered his vision. The clearing in the background was in the forest outside

Stentis. He quickly gave the dog one last pat and mounted the black horse. He turned and galloped through the forest.

"I'm coming, Thresi," he thought as the wind brushed against his face.

14

A Cup of Bad Memories

THE MORNING WAS bathed in golden sunlight. Thresi had slept near Atlas, but the first rays of dawn had woken her. After eating some meat, drinking some water, and having his bandages changed, Atlas had fallen asleep. Thresi had many questions, but she decided to wait until morning. Tiger was up and cooking breakfast. Atlas was sitting against a tree with Katan still asleep by his side. Sparks and Zatern were hunting in the forest. Sleepily, Thresi stood up and walked toward Atlas. She wanted answers, and she was going to get them one way or another.

Atlas was just staring at the clearing. He had no emotion in his eyes, just a blank stare that made Thresi's heart fill with sorrow.

"Stompina, Atlas," Thresi said cheerfully.

Atlas smiled at the sound of his own language.

"Stompina to you, too, Thresi. Now what

questions do you have?" Atlas asked in a casual tone.

Thresi couldn't believe he knew what she was up to.

"Don't be shocked," he said. "I read your mind while you were walking toward me."

"How did you manage that?" Thresi asked excitedly. "Is that how you knew I was contacting Sparks in Stentis?"

"Yes, it's a Guardian trick," said Atlas. "It's just about the only thing we have besides dragons. Though, Rogues have a certain type of empathy, and Zodiacs have instincts. But only Guardians can read minds."

"But Katan told me that only your dragon can read your mind," Thresi protested.

"Just between you and me, don't believe a word Katan says while he's drinking, eating, or sleeping," said Atlas, smiling. "He'll tell you anything just so you'll leave him alone."

After hearing about his arm, he had felt depressed.

Thresi smiled back at him and said, "Well, you answered one of my questions. Now answer this—" Thresi's voice then turned grave. "How did you know those Vampires? I mean, I knew Otto because he dated my sister and later killed her. But you knew all three."

Atlas just stared at her without any expression on his face. He drew his blanketed knees up to his chest and rested his head on them. He hugged them the best he could with his right arm and sighed. Something about this sight made Thresi wish she had never brought up the subject.

"Do you really want to know? It's a very gruesome story, and I'd hate to scare you," he said in a low, sad voice.

Thresi nodded her head and sat down in front of him.

"I was twelve, and it was summer, the worst time for my clan," said Atlas. "We lived near a huge volcano range that separated the East Coast from the Plains of Fire. Dorande means 'volcano.' Some Vampires lived on the other side of the range. One day, the Vampires came over the volcano range and attacked us. It was pandemonium! My family hid anywhere the Vampires wouldn't find us. Most of the members of my clan were killed. Every second, I had to watch and see my friends and family get killed and wringed dry of every ounce of blood in their lifeless bodies. It started to die down until those three Vampires came. They slew left and right, killing and eating anyone, until they eventually got my parents, leaving me and your mother, who was twenty-five, alive. The three of them tried to get us, but our uncle sacrificed himself for us. They left. The original population of my clan was down to 100 from 500."

Atlas continued, "I did the one thing that Rogue boys were never to do. I cried. I was so hysterical about the loss of my clan that I couldn't contain myself. Your mother tried to calm me down, but it didn't work. I was punished for it. Because I cried, I showed weakness, and our clan leader beat me because of it. Your mother tried to heal me, but the scars didn't heal right, so they are a living memory all over my body. We lived together in a small hut at the edge of our clan as it started to rebuild."

Atlas finished with a quiet tone. He turned his head away, and his shoulders shook.

Thresi's eyes were watery, and she said sincerely, "I am so sorry. Atlas. You didn't have to tell me."

"Well now you know," he said quickly.

"My mother told a similar story to Milo, but that happened 106 years ago. How old are you?" Thresi asked, astonished.

Atlas looked at her and said, "118. If you don't mind, I'd like to be alone."

Thresi waved good-bye as she walked to where Tiger was eating a peach.

Tiger asked, "He told you about the massacre of the Dorande clan, didn't he?"

Thresi nodded her head and responded, "The worst part is that he got beaten for mourning over his loss."

Tiger nodded her head and handed Thresi some fruit. She said, "I don't believe in the way that Rogues act, but they do everything for a reason."

Thresi nodded her head again.

Tiger said, "I've decided to start your training."

Thresi nodded and asked, "Tiger, if Atlas is 118, then how old are you?"

Tiger replied, "116."

The day was slow, nobody did a thing , and the dragons returned. Atlas didn't eat anything. The only time he acknowledged them was when they changed his bandages. When the moon rose, Thresi went to sleep, snuggling next to Sparks.

15

ADD ESSENCE OF KNOWLEDGE

A HAND VIGOROUSLY SHAKING Thresi woke her up.

"Come on. Get up," Atlas said as he kept shaking her. "Do you want to start your training or no?"

Thresi opened her eyes groggily, allowing light to trickle into her pupils. She sat up and asked, "Are you training me, Atlas?"

Atlas shook his head and pointed to Tiger.

"I'm trying to get my strength back by exercising," Atlas said.

Then he turned around and ran into the forest with Katan flying above him. Thresi walked toward Tiger, who was sitting by the fire.

Thresi sat down and asked, "Where do we begin, Tiger?"

"We begin with mind-reading," Tiger said. "But we need to work on your defenses. Think of some defense, like a wall, so you can guard portions of your mind, like memories. But be careful not to guard with the information your enemy might want."

They practiced for over an hour. When Tiger got into Thresi's mind, she'd leave Zodian or Roguish words in her conquest. After two hours of work, Thresi finally managed to block Tiger. So they moved on to the next lesson, which was getting into the mind. It only took half the time because Tiger weakened her defense so Thresi would have an easier time. Every time Thresi was successful, Tiger would strengthen her defenses. They continued to learn what to do when someone entered Thresi's mind. Tiger taught her how to set her mind on fire, the simplest, non-painful thing Thresi could do.

Tiger also taught her Roguish and Zodian maneuvers Thresi could do while fighting on a dragon. Sparks and Zatern worked with Thresi on flying maneuvers, which Thresi excelled at. This training continued for four days.

Those days went fast for everyone. With the training, packing, running, and flying, no one had any free time. On the fifth day, after a rigorous training session, Tiger, Zatern, Thresi, and Sparks went into the forest to scavenge for healing herbs for their trip to Stomio.

"Thresi, you're great in your lessons, but those are only the basics," Tiger said in a happy tone.

"The same goes to you, Sparks," Zatern added in his deep voice.

"I can't wait until we get Stomio and see the other dragons. I just can't wait!" Sparks yelled.

Thresi rubbed Sparks' neck.

"Yes, it will be exciting. Tiger, how long do you think it will take?" Thresi asked while picking up a red snake plant.

"It will probably take ten days to get to the city of Edron. A Zodian boat should be waiting for us. Then we'll take a three-week trip over the Blitic Sea. We should arrive in the middle of summer," Tiger replied.

They continued picking up herbs and practicing the other languages until Atlas bound out of the forest, dragging someone in cloak. Katan was right behind him.

"Thresi," Atlas said in an annoyed tone, "is this Human yours? He claims to know you."

Thresi walked toward the stranger and removed the hood. There stood Milo. He was smiling even though he was caked in dirt and his hair was disheveled.

"Milo!" Thresi yelled happily and hugged him. Atlas let go of Milo's arm so he could hug her. "Why are you here and not in Trenton?"

She put her hand on his right shoulder. He flinched from the pressure that Thresi put on his sore wound.

"I'm so glad I found you before you left Quint. Are you all right? You had me worried sick!" Milo said, looking over Thresi.

"I'm fine," she said, stopping her brother's frantic movements. "I'm not the one who flinched when someone touched my shoulder."

Milo smiled and stared at her.

"So how has Trenton fared since I've been gone?" Thresi asked.

Milo told her everything that happened. Atlas and Katan stood next to Zatern, Tiger, and Sparks.

Atlas turned to Tiger and said, "I have a sneaking suspicion that they're related."

Tiger nodded her head. She noted that Thresi and Milo talked the same way and used the same hand gestures. When Milo told the story of the Vampire, Thresi looked toward Atlas and Tiger, but they decided to let Milo continue.

"So Nera led me to this clearing, where I remembered my vision. I took off to come here," Milo finished.

Thresi stared at him and said, "That Vampire you met is named Trip. I didn't think they'd come after you."

Atlas scratched his head and said, "It seems they only want information, but I'm sure you being an All-Seer has something to do it."

Milo stared at Thresi and whispered, "Who are these people?"

Thresi laughed at him. Stifling a giggle, she said, "Forgive me for being rude." She turned and gestured toward Atlas. "This is Atlas of the Dorande clan. A Rogue Guardian."

"He looks a lot like our mom," Milo said, surprised.

Thresi laughed again and said, "He's our uncle. Our mother's little brother."

Milo looked at Atlas and said, "Nice to meet

you Atlas of the Dorande clan. I'm Milo, Thresi's older brother."

They clasped arms.

"Nice to meet you, too, Milo, my sister's son," Atlas said in a happy tone.

Thresi turned to Milo and gestured toward Katan, who was eyeing Milo with a criticizing gaze.

"This is Katan, Atlas' dragon," she said.

Katan moved his head closer to Milo and said with distaste, "Why are Humans so short? How do you people live?"

"Quite easily actually," Milo said in a matter-of-fact tone.

Katan scowled at him and moved his head away. Atlas laughed and patted Katan's large shoulder.

"Wow, you really are my nephew. Not many people can make a good comeback to Katan," Atlas said, still laughing.

"And this is Tiger the Zodiac. She's also a Guardian. The red dragon to her right is Zatern," Thresi said.

Like a gentleman, Milo bowed toward Tiger and said, "Very mice to meet you, Tiger."

Tiger bowed her head. Without any emotion, she said, "Likewise."

Zatern bowed his head toward Milo. Thresi turned toward Sparks, who was nearly exploding from excitement.

"Remember the thing under my dress?" Thresi asked.

Milo nodded his head.

"That's her," Thresi said, pointing toward Sparks.

Milo looked to where Thresi was pointing and gaped at the site of the giant green dragon.

"Hi, I'm Sparks," Sparks' soft female voice said happily.

Milo just stared at Sparks and said, "Thresi, how did you fit her in your dress? She's huge!"

Thresi laughed and said, "She was a baby back then."

"That makes much more sense. It's nice to meet you, Sparks," he said, bowing to Sparks.

She laughed in enjoyment.

"You must be hungry, Milo. Come eat with us," Tiger said.

So they went and ate by the fire, talking during the night. Eventually, Atlas and Tiger retired into sleep while Milo and Thresi exchanged more stories. Thresi explained everything that had happened and what a Guardian was. They eventually went to sleep.

"I'm glad Milo is back," Thresi thought as she drifted to sleep.

16

A Pint of Storm

THE ROLL OF distant thunder, not the sunlight, woke up Thresi. She sat up. It was almost as dark as night. She carefully stood up so as not to wake up Milo. She walked to the middle of the clearing. Another roll of thunder passed loudly overhead. Tiger and Zatern landed in front of her.

"Phew," Tiger said, exhausted, "This storm is huge, but, luckily, it's not too bad to fly in. Thresi, Atlas is finishing packing. Could you go help him? I'm going to see if we should fly through it or not."

Zatern shook his body. Beads of water flew from his scaly body.

"Wake up your brother and Sparks, too, Thresi. It will probably be best if we left as soon as possible," Zatern said, stretching his neck. He took off from a standstill.

Thresi jogged back to the campsite with thunder booming all around. She stood in front of a sleeping Milo. Thresi remembered that he was difficult to wake, so she gave him a good kick in his wounded shoulder.

"Ouch!" Milo yelped. "Why did you do that? That was my bad shoulder!"

"Sorry, but it was either kick you or spend twenty minutes trying to shake you awake," Thresi replied causally. "Now get up. Come on."

Milo stood up and brushed himself off.

"All right! You're bossy. You know that, right?" Milo said, annoyed.

Thresi giggled and thought, "Sparks, are you awake?"

"Of course I am. I was watching you and Milo. I like him. He's a boy version of you," Sparks said, giggling. She got up and stretched.

"We need to help Atlas pack up the campsite. We're leaving soon," Thresi said.

"You are definitely bossy," Milo said jokingly.

They both laughed as they walked toward Atlas and Katan, who were in hurried rush. The thunder was getting louder with every step.

"I was wondering when you guys would help us pack," Atlas said, upset. "We haven't gotten some things over by that tree."

Thunder continued to roll over their heads as they packed the food and supplies. Suddenly, Tiger and Zatern landed in fury of wind and water.

"Quickly! We must leave now before this storm gets worse," Tiger yelled as the rain started to pour down. “Load the things on the dragons now!”

Everyone scurried to load his or her things on the dragons. Except for Milo, everyone soon mounted his or her dragon.

“My horse ran away. I can’t follow you,” he said with despair.

Thresi turned toward Milo and smiled. She said sternly, “You’re going to ride with me, Milo. I’d never leave you behind!”

Sparks lowered herself so Milo could get on behind Thresi.

“You do know how to fly her, right?” Milo asked nervously.

Thresi ignored him and prepped herself for takeoff.

“Stay close to me, Thresi,” Atlas said, riding Katan.

They took off into the air. Milo quickly squeezed his arms around Thresi as they flew into the storm.

The storm seemed mild on the ground, but anything on the ground seemed to be mild. In the sky, the storm was filled with strong, impassable wind. Thick blobs of rain felt like rocks when they came in contact with flesh or scales. The group was faring well. The rain was drenching the group. Thunder continued to roll, but it was almost deafening now.

“Thresi!” yelled Milo over the thunder.

“What is it?!” Thresi answered loudly.

“Lightning!” yelled Milo during the loudest roll of thunder Thresi had ever heard. She saw the bolt of lightning flash by Katan's left flank. A strand of lightning hit Atlas' shoulder. Atlas moaned in pain and flew to Sparks' side.

"Are you all right, Atlas?" Sparks asked over the pounding of rain.

"I'm fine, but this isn't your average thunderstorm," he replied, rubbing his left shoulder.

"Then what is it?" Milo and Thresi yelled in unison.

"An energy storm. Guardians ride into these storms and collect the energy in special shields. Because there aren't any Human Guardians, energy storms are much more prominent in Quint," Atlas said.

"We should get out of here!" Milo called.

"We can't. Look below you," Atlas said.

Thresi and Milo both looked down and saw the clouds. Giant streams of endless energy weaving through each other connected the billows.

"If you enter that, you will die," said Atlas. "Little strands like the one that got me will burn, but not kill you."

"We have to avoid this energy at all costs, don't we?" Sparks asked.

A flash of energy passed in the space between Sparks and Katan. A large strand hit Milo in his wounded shoulder. Milo screamed in pain as liquid fire burned at his wounded flesh.

"Don't worry, Milo! We'll be out of here in no time!" Thresi called to him.

Energy flashed in front of Sparks as she did

a forward roll to avoid it. But a little strand got Thresi on one of her hands that held Sparks' neck spikes. She winced in pain as the energy singed her flesh. Atlas maneuvered away from another flash. Thresi heard Atlas grunt. It seemed there was no escape from the energy tendrils.

All three dragons moved with great speed and agility to protect their riders from the burn of energy. Zatern grunted with pain as a tendril nicked his neck.

"It will be all right, Zatern. We shall get out of this," Tiger said, patting his neck.

Tiger had been struck many times, leaving her skin feeling as if it was on constant fire. The others were not faring well either. It felt like an hour had passed. Atlas's body was filled with pain as Katan swerved out of the way of an oncoming energy stream.

"This is getting bad, Katan," Atlas thought, frowning.

"Yes, it is. We need to get out!" Katan thought.

The three dragons came side by side after another energy stream passed by.

"We need to leave this storm or else," Tiger yelled over a roll of thunder.

"But how do we get out of this?" Thresi asked tiredly.

"Our only exit leads to death," Milo said nervously.

"I bet we can make it through the bottom if we're quick about it," Atlas said confidently.

"But you said it leads to certain death," Milo protested.

"I didn't say certain death," Atlas replied, smiling.

"You know he's right," Thresi added.

"All right! All right! You win. Let's all go get killed!" Milo yelled, feeling defeated.

"I believe I found a passage through," Tiger called to them as her hands moved in a pattern. "Just follow me."

Zatern turned and did a nosedive into the fray of energy. Sparks and Katan quickly followed. The wind whipped at Thresi's face. Milo gripped Thresi harder as they plummeted toward the earth. Energy flashed before them, and its tendrils burned as the dragons slowly dropped in altitude. It took a matter of minutes before they spotted ground. The dragons leveled their flight and quickly landed on the ground. The rain still pounded on, and the energy flashed above them. The dragons lay down, and the riders flopped off. The dragons used their wings to shield the Guardians. The group was battered, burned, and wet. The pain helped them drifted off to sleep.

17

Add Some New Supplies

THE MORNING WAS bright and sunny. Almost anyone would think it was a wondrous day, except for an All-Seer and the three Guardians, who spent their morning healing their overwhelming amount of burns.

"Ouch! Ouch! Ouch! Stop that, Tiger! It hurts like crazy!" Atlas yelled as Tiger dabbed a wet cloth over the burns on his left arm.

The arm just hung there. Thresi knew that, if Atlas could use it, he would jerk it away from Tiger.

"Oh, don't be such a baby, Atlas. Thresi had more guts than you," Tiger replied mockingly.

Tiger had healed Thresi first. Burns had covered most of Thresi's body, but, thanks to Tiger's special burn ointment, they all pretty much disappeared. Milo had been next. While she healed his burns, Tiger healed his shoulder. Atlas was a little nervous about getting his burns treated. Thresi could understand why. It seemed that any liquid on the burn caused more pain than the burn itself. Out of sheer kindness, Tiger wanted to heal everyone before herself.

"I'm not being a baby, Tiger. You seem rather cranky this morning," Atlas replied coolly.

"I'm cranky for many reasons," said Tiger. "One of which is that our supplies and food got completely incinerated in the storm."

Tiger was right. The storm completely destroyed their belongings, except for what they wore on their backs, which were Milo and Thresi's cloaks, their weapons, and a few of Tiger's healing herbs. Luckily, those included the ones that healed burns.

"I'm sure we can get more supplies. There's sure to be a town around here," Thresi said reassuringly.

"I have a map," Milo piped up.

"You have a map," Atlas answered, "but no food."

"Exactly," Milo answered.

Tiger put Atlas' arm back in its sling and started to tend to her own wounds.

"See that mountain over there," Milo continued. "That's Johnny's Foot." He took out the map and pointed to a large triangle. "We are probably here." He pointed at a clearing. Everyone was gathered around the map. "So the nearest town is Clot, and it's at least a mile away."

Tiger looked at the map and pointed toward Edron. She said happily, "So Edron is about a seven-day flight, which means we're making good time."

"So we should start walking if we want to eat soon," Atlas suggested.

"Where should we meet you, Tiger?" Thresi asked.

"It seems the forest outside of the town is completely devoid of the road. So meet me there," Tiger answered, putting away her healing herbs.

Suddenly, the dragons landed in a fury of wind.

"What's wrong, you three?" Thresi asked, moving toward Sparks.

"I smelled blood," Zatern said nervously.

They all seemed jittery to Thresi. She tried to touch Sparks' shoulder, but Sparks tensed at her touch.

"Dead bodies litter the forest," said Katan. "They are pale and shriveled, showing signs of all the blood being wringed out of their bodies. I believe that—"

Katan couldn't finish his statement before Sparks said creepily, "They're back."

Thresi gasped as she realized what Sparks was saying. The three nightmares from Stentis were making their way toward the group. It seemed that the Vampires were having a huge feast on the poor farmers who lived in the area.

"The good news is that, if anyone did see us, he or she didn't get the chance to tell anyone," Atlas said with uncertainty.

Atlas always seemed to find the best out of anything or anyone, except for himself. No doubt, his self-insecurity was a result of the many beatings he received from his clan after the massacre. Nonetheless, he was one of the greatest optimists.

"They probably were questioned before they were killed," Tiger said.

Like most Zodiacs, Tiger was a realist, but they could sometimes be philosophers. Rogues were mostly pessimists.

"We need to leave now. They could be waiting in the forest, waiting for us to sleep and be completely unaware," Thresi said nervously.

"Let's go forth to the town," Milo said.

Tiger mounted Zatern, and they launched into the sky with Katan and Sparks. The others quickly headed into the forest.

The forest was filled with the smell of moisture. Thresi's hands brushed against the wet leaves of the trees as she walked on the wood grove's path.

"It's so beautiful after a rainstorm with the plants and grass coated with dew. It's like poetry," Thresi said, rubbing a leaf in her hands. "The storm is usually beautiful, too."

"Everything is beautiful on the ground, especially if you aren't experiencing it," Atlas said over his shoulder.

"Do you like Quint, Atlas? I mean, better than Arsine?" Thresi asked, starting to collect leaves from the trees.

"You never know when you'll need a leaf," she thought.

"I do like Quint better than Arsine. Quint has everything that Arsine doesn't," Atlas replied.

Atlas ran his hands down the bark of a birch tree.

"Like trees?" Milo asked with his eyes closed.

"Like trees. How did you know that?" Atlas asked over his shoulder.

Milo smiled, opened his eyes, and answered, "I had a vision of Arsine while you and Thresi were talking."

"Now I'm definitely sure you are an All-Seer," Atlas called.

The village was up ahead. They saw a tree with a sign on it. Thresi put her leaves in her sleeve, walked up to the tree, and took down the poster. She slowly studied it.

"What does it say?" Milo asked.

"By the order of King Strot, all All-Seers are to report to the capital city of Createna. Soldiers of the king's guard will capture all who fail to do so. If anyone sees a person with dull, gray eyes, tell any solider immediately."

"Wow!" Thresi said, crumpling the poster and throwing it into the forest.

"My eyes are not dull. They're stormy," Milo complained.

Atlas thumped him on the head.

"Ow!" said Milo.

"Don't draw any attention to yourself. We're in enough trouble as it is," Atlas whispered. "But how do we get out of it?"

Atlas thought for moment. Then his eyes brightened. He took Milo's cloak and ripped a long strip from it. He walked into the forest for a moment and came back with a long stick.

"How comfortable are you with playing a blind man?" Atlas asked Milo.

"Not very. I'd personally prefer not to," Milo said uneasily. "But I have to, don't I?"

"Yep," Atlas replied.

He gave Milo the strip and stick. Milo tied the strip of cloth over his eyes and held the walking stick in his right hand.

"Now which one of you is going to lead me?" Milo asked, smiling.

"I'll lead you, blind bat," Thresi replied, laughing.

They linked arms and walked ahead with Atlas close behind.

18

A Tablespoon of Danger

TIGER SAT DOWN hard on the grass. Zatern, Sparks, and Katan sat anxiously on the ground.

"We're so close to Edron, Tiger. I can feel it," Sparks said excitedly.

"Do you want to know what I'm feeling?" Katan asked. "Extreme hunger."

"Why don't you guys go hunt? I'll be all right," Tiger said.

Zatern stared at the forest.

"Something isn't right," he thought.

Katan and Sparks were all ready airborne.

"Go on, Zatern," Tiger said reassuringly. "I'll be all right."

Zatern nodded his head and flew off after the others. Tiger started to meditate with the sounds of nature buzzing around her.

"Well, well, well, if it isn't the lone Zodiac," a voice mocked from within the thick forest growth.

Tiger immediately stood and drew her two short swords. Otto, Somari, and Trip emerged from the forest, brandishing their blood red daggers. They were laughing their evil, malice cackles.

"Where are your friends, Tiger? Surely they didn't go and abandon you?" Somari's cunning voice asked.

Tiger gripped her swords tighter and said, "No, they didn't. If you don't leave, I'll kill you." Venom dripped from her words.

"Oh, we're so scared!" Trip said sarcastically, "Like you'd kill us."

"So we'll make you a deal," Otto said, musing. "If you tell us where Thresi is, we'll let you live. We might even let Atlas live."

"You're so generous," Tiger said mockingly, "but I'm leaning toward the option of killing you."

"Suit yourself," Otto said.

All three Vampires charged toward Tiger. She crossed her blades as the daggers were thrust at her chest. The Vampires formed a triangle around the Guardian. Trip and Somari were fighting Tiger from her sides, leaving her open to Otto's frontal attack. Otto moved his blade quickly toward her, but he was too slow for Tiger, who moved her left sword to block.

The Vampires recoiled in anger because their plan didn't work. They moved into a line and attacked at once. Tiger moved her swords to block the red blades, but Otto's blade was able to pierce the flesh of her shoulder. Tiger winced in pain as the blue blood of Zodiacs leaked out of the wound. The Vampires grinned wickedly because they knew they had weakened Tiger's defense. They pushed onward, forming the triangle position. Tiger defended herself from her side attackers. She was expecting Otto to attack her again, but he didn't. He threw his dagger toward Tiger's head, but, instead of the blade hitting her head, the hilt did, rendering her unconscious. Tiger's swords fell to the ground as she staggered and hit the ground.

Somari was about to kill her when Trip called, "Wait! Don't kill her!"

Somari and Otto glanced at him strangely. "Don't you see? We use her as bait to lure Thresi into our clutches. Maybe her brother, too."

"What about Atlas and the dragons?" Somari asked.

"We don't have to worry about the dragons. They won't attack when we have their Guardians. And Atlas can be a great meal."

They all laughed as Otto got some rope. He bound Tiger's hands and threw her over his shoulder.

"What do we do with Tiger after we have what we want?" Otto asked, shifting Tiger to his other shoulder.

"Because we can't eat her, we'll give her to Quess as a gift," Trip answered.

The Vampires slowly walked toward their camp, making sure they left signs so the others could follow them.

19

Stir in a Fortune Reading

THRESI CAREFULLY LEAD Milo through the streets of Clot. People were staring at them, but they'd back off when Atlas flashed them a smile. Thresi gathered that Atlas' perfectly pointed teeth scared them off.

"I have a question," Milo said, staring in front of him. "Do we have any money?"

Atlas stopped walking and searched his belt for his money bag. "Drat! We don't have any. I knew I shouldn't have put it in my bedroll," Atlas said angrily.

"Perhaps someone needs work to be done," Thresi said thoughtfully.

"I couldn't help but overhear your problem," said a voice.

Thresi turned to see a lady with a hood over her eyes.

"I need someone to watch my tent for a while. I need to take care of my sick husband. I will pay you well."

Thresi locked eyes with the woman and said, "We would love to help you."

"Then come into my tent," said the woman.

Thresi led Milo into the dark tent with Atlas taking the rear. The tent was filled with strange crystal balls and lucky charms. Tarot decks were on a shelf next to an oversized book.

"In case you haven't guessed, I'm a soothsayer, but you can call me Meg," she said, taking down her hood to reveal stormy, gray eyes. She gestured toward Milo. "Your friend is in good company."

"So you're an All-Seer too?" Milo asked, smiling.

"Yes," Meg replied. "Now, if you get any customers, make up some answer. It shall do for now. Many times, when people don't get the answer they want, they forget it."

They nodded toward Meg as she put her hood back over her eyes and left the tent.

"Why doesn't she just put up a closed sign instead of asking random people off the street to watch her tent?" Atlas asked, looking through one of the many tarot decks.

"Soothsayers can't just close their business. They're supposed to be open all the time," Milo stated.

"You guys, someone is coming," Thresi called nervously.

Thresi quickly sat in a chair that was near a table that held a crystal ball. She was assuming the role of soothsayer. The man looked like a poor farmer. He had heavy, tanned skin with gray hair peeking its way through his black hair. His face was filled with sadness. His face pulled Thresi's heartstrings. The farmer sat down in the chair across form Thresi.

"Madame Soothsayer, my son is very sick. Will he get better?" the old farmer asked.

Thresi was speechless. She expected the people who would come to the tent would have petty problems, not serious ones like a sick son.

When Milo heard this question, he knew he should answer it, not Thresi. He could give a true answer while Thresi could only make up something. Milo focused on the man's question, but he couldn't see anything. He realized he didn't know who he was looking for. He needed to look at the man. Milo's hands moved toward the blindfold over his eyes. He undid the knot on the back, and the blindfold fell down into his outstretched hand. Milo quickly glanced at the old man and closed his eyes.

A vision of a woman crying over a boy about his age with a deathly pale face filled his head. The old farmer stood also over the son, weeping softly. It seemed like a week passed in the vision. The woman opened her door and picked up a baby that was left on their doorstep. Milo knew it was a baby boy.

The vision ended, and Milo opened his eyes. He stared at the farmer and watched as Thresi tried to make up an answer.

Milo stepped forward and said, "Your son will die, but do not grieve too harshly. In a week's time, you will receive a baby boy at your doorstep."

The farmer and Milo locked eyes for a moment, but the farmer pulled away from Milo's impenetrable gaze.

"Thank you, sir," the farmer said, frowning. "For the sake of my family, I hope you are wrong."

But the farmer knew Milo wasn't wrong. He knew Milo was an All-Seer. The farmer bowed and left the tent in a huff.

There was silence in the tent before Thresi asked, "Did you really see all that Milo?"

Milo nodded his head.

Atlas shook his and said, "You shouldn't have done that, Milo. That man might go tell a soldier or someone about you."

"I don't think that poor man will do any thing of the sort, Atlas," Thresi said sternly.

"I hate to tell you, Thresi, but Milo didn't really give that man any good news," Atlas replied.

Atlas was right. The farmer immediately told a soldier, who was very close to the tent. Footsteps approached the tent.

Atlas was the first to sense the soldiers' presence coming toward them. "It seems I was right, you two," Atlas said pridefully. "But they aren't that close, so we still can still get away."

The group immediately left the tent. They walked down the street at a brisk pace.

It wasn't long before a voice called, "Hey! Stop where you are!"

Thresi turned to see about twenty soldiers chasing after them.

"You guys, we have a problem!" Thresi called to the boys in the lead.

Atlas and Milo looked back at the mass of soldiers heading their way toward them.

"Drat! Run!" Atlas yelled.

They took off in a sprint, but so did the soldiers. They ran as fast as their legs could carry them, but the soldiers still gained. Soon, the group came to a corner leading into an alley. As they turned, the soldiers started to disappear. They stopped in the middle of the alleyway.

"I think we're safe," Atlas said as they caught their breath.

"Not quite," a voice said.

Swords were then pointed at their chins.

"Tie them up," the voice called again.

Before Atlas, Thresi, or Milo could do anything, their hands were tied behind their backs, and they were thrown into a cart. Soon, a heavy, black sheet was pulled over them.

20

A Touch of Drat

IT SEEMED LIKE they were in that cart for hours. Thresi tried to stay calm and contact Sparks, but her mind was too worried about what was happening and would not stay in focus. Thresi could tell Milo was nervous. His breath was long and shallow. Atlas, as it seemed, was asleep.

"How could he sleep at a time like this?" Thresi thought.

She really wanted to kick him awake, but that probably wouldn't help the situation. The cart suddenly stopped, and she heard what sounded like someone running approaching the cart.

"Sirs! Sirs! I am a messenger from the town of Sypheres," cried a panicked voice of a boy. He must have been no older than Thresi. "The town's All-Seers are leading a revolt. They have successfully overpowered the soldiers stationed there. They need reinforcements!"

"Don't worry, boy. We will come to Sypheres' aid," said the voice of their captor.

"General," said a husky voice, "what of the prisoners in the back?"

"I know someone in the area who can take them to Createna," the general replied. "Wait here, boy. We'll be back soon."

Soon, the cart was in motion, giving Thresi an uneasy feeling about who they were about to be handed off to. Thresi looked toward Milo.

He looked asleep, but he turned toward Thresi and whispered, "Thresi, Tiger has been taken! I tried looking for her in the clearing. We were supposed to meet her, but she was gone. I tried to look for her, but I couldn't find her."

"Don't worry Milo. We'll find her, but we have our own problems right now," Thresi replied calmly.

She waited for Milo to reply, but all she heard was his nervous breaths. She tried to contact Tiger, but, yet again, her mind started thinking of a strategy to escape instead of trying to clear her mind. She let it do as it pleased. As ideas flowed through her head, she realized the guards hadn't disarmed them.

"Yes! Score one for the good guys," she thought.

Even with their weapons, they still had the ropes to deal with and the number of guards. It was best to wait until they were handed off. Soon, Thresi was drifting into sleep, dreaming of her plan.

Thresi soon woke to something nudging

her. She turned her head to see Atlas nudging her with his head.

Thresi turned over to face him and asked, "What is it?"

"I read one of the soldier's thoughts. He was a bit clueless, but I was able to find something out. Thresi, they're taking us to Otto and company!" Atlas whispered loudly.

Thresi didn't know how take this news. For one thing, the whole group knew the Vampires had been tracking them, but she thought the storm would have covered their trails.

Milo rolled over and whispered, "This is a good thing!"

Thresi and Atlas looked at Milo like he was crazy.

"How?" they asked in unison.

"Because the Vampires have Tiger. We go to them, we find her," Milo explained like it was blatantly obvious.

Thresi nodded her head in agreement. Atlas looked at both of them worriedly and confusedly.

"Since when?" he asked.

"Atlas, you are so out of the loop," Thresi said jokingly.

She expected him to laugh, but he looked grave and serious instead.

"You're really worried, aren't you?" Milo asked. His gray eyes had a sad glint.

Atlas nodded his head. Tears were brimming in his eyes.

"We've been friends ever since I was an apprentice Guardian," he replied.

But the conversation ended when the wagon bumped into a root.

Milo shivered, closed his eyes, and said, "We're really close now." He opened his eyes. "Never mind. We're here."

21

A Quart of Promise

Tiger turned her head toward the opening of Vampire's camp. Her tiger like senses picked up on the sound of a cart wheeling toward her on the soft forest floor. Tiger tried to turn her body, but the ropes that bound her to a tree would not yield.

"Stop your squirming, Zodiac," Otto called as he got more rope.

"What's he doing?" Tiger thought.

She turned her head to see Trip making his way toward her with bottles and rags. He knelt beside her and rolled up her sleeve to reveal the horrible slash on her shoulder. He ran his fingers over the marred skin.

"I'm sorry my friend did this to you. The Vampires did have a pact with the Zodiacs, but since it was proven void, all's fair. Though, I prefer to keep any promise," Trip said, smiling and showing his fangs.

Tiger raised her eyebrow at him, "The only

reason we even made the pact was because you couldn't eat us.". Trip poured some of the bottle's contents on a rag and rubbed the wound with smooth, but firm, strokes.

"True I admit but even when Quess attacked a Zodian boat no one was hurt."

"Why are you helping me?" Tiger asked sternly.

"Did I not just say that I respect promises? Besides, you'll need to be as healthy as you can to save your friends," Trip said. A sly smile formed on his lips.

"What do you mean?" Tiger asked angrily.

Trip laughed softly as he rubbed the rag over Tiger's wound.

"Isn't it obvious? The cart that's coming has your friends in it. Lord Salvarn, Quess' brother, captured them in Clot. He was in the area. Because news about Thresi spread like wildfire through the Vampire community, it was only a matter of time before she was caught."

"But why would you want me to save them? Don't you want her caught?" Tiger asked.

"If I had been born a Vampire, sure. Because I wasn't, I really don't want to see the Humans fall," Trip stated as he stopped rubbing Tiger's wound.

"You weren't born a Vampire?" Tiger asked.

Trip just shook his head and pulled out his dagger.

"That's a story I don't want to tell," he said, cutting the rope that held Tiger to the tree. "It's best you leave now and hide in the trees or contact your dragons."

Tiger turned to leave, but Trip grabbed her hand. His hand was cold against Tiger's warm skin.

He said, "Promise me that you won't forget what I did just now, no matter what I have to do in the future."

"I promise, Trip. I won't forget what you did for the world today," Tiger said with sincerity.

Trip let go off her hand. Her warmth disappeared from his cold skin. Then Tiger ran toward the cover of the forest.

22

A Smidge of Surprise

THE CART STOPPED. Thresi was pulled from the cart and forced to stand. Thresi quickly scanned for Tiger, but she could only find a pile of rope.

"I was wrong. I thought she was here!" Milo said angrily as he was pulled next to Thresi. Thresi turned to see a soldier try to grab Atlas, but Atlas bared his teeth and walked himself toward Thresi.

"Then where is she?" Atlas asked.

Milo didn't say anything. He just hung his head in shame. The three Vampires walked toward the group. Thresi noticed that Trip wasn't grinning wickedly like the others. He had more of a sad, longing face.

"Well, what a wonderful surprise. It seems we've gotten exactly what we wanted," Somari said happily. She turned toward Lord Salvarn. "Thank you for finding them, my lord. We will repay you."

Lord Salvarn just nodded his head and turned away, but he called over his shoulder, "Good-bye. Remember what will happen if you fail."

He climbed onto the cart as the pitch-black horses picked up a gallop and disappeared into the forest. Otto walked toward them and smiled wickedly.

"Welcome to our modest campsite. It may not be what your used to, but don't fret. You won't have to stay here long," Otto said mockingly.

Trip grabbed Milo by his arm and tied him to a tree. Otto did the same for Thresi. Somari grabbed Atlas and forced him to kneel.

"Leave him alone!" Thresi yelled at Somari as she struggled against the tree.

For some strange reason, her hands started to feel a hot, burning sensation that filled her blood with liquid fire as her temper raised. Soon, the burning ceased, but pain replaced it. Otto laughed with malice as he got a coil of rope that had a strange glow to it.

"What a shame you haven't been properly trained, Thresi. Perhaps you could actually leave this camp alive, but, sadly, you and your friends must suffer," Otto said mockingly.

Somari and Trip just chuckled quietly to themselves. Thresi turned her face away and looked at Milo directly in his eyes.

"Milo," Thresi said telepathically, "we need a way out. They're going to kill Atlas I know it."

"I know, but these Vampires are really good at tying knots," Milo replied telepathically.

Atlas fought against Trip and Somari as they held him down. Otto tied the glowing rope around him. Thresi noticed that Atlas' hands were starting to glow. Thresi knew they were hot enough to burn the rope, but they didn't. The rope was left unfazed.

"I'm afraid your fire won't work on those ropes, Atlas," Trip said chidingly.

Atlas' hands stopped glowing, but he kept struggling. Milo turned his head and looked into the forest.

"What is it, Milo?" Thresi asked.

"Tiger!" he thought.

"Milo, what do you mean?" Thresi asked.

But Milo didn't respond. As if in a trance, he kept looking into the forest. Thresi felt something tug at her ropes. She turned to see glowing, green eyes emerge from the bush. It took all of her willpower not to scream.

"Relax, Thresi. It's me, Tiger," she whispered.

The ropes fell off of Thresi's hands.

"Come inside the bush. I have already saved Milo. The dragons are just outside the forest. I'll save Atlas," said Tiger.

"No, I will," Thresi whispered. "This is very random, but you should steal the Vampires' supplies. They probably will be lost without them.

Tiger closed her eyes. Thresi thought she heard a low growl come from the bush.

"All right. But only because I trust your fighting skill. I suppose this is your battle anyway. Be careful of the rope. It is very dangerous as well as extremely thick. Best you don't try to cut it," Tiger said.

But her voice soon disappeared. Thresi stood up, drew her sword, and slowly walked to a bush near the main camp and waited.

An hour passed. Soon, Thresi emerged from the bush, only to see Atlas leaning against a tree while rubbing the blade of his sword. A strange, black substance was all over the ground. It reeked with the smell of death.

"I was wondering when you might see it fit to come out of that bush," he said with his usual strange smile.

"Atlas," Thresi said, groaning, "I was supposed to rescue you. Not the other way around!"

Thresi sheathed her sword and crossed her arms. Atlas just laughed.

"I didn't save myself. I actually had a little help," Atlas paused for a second. "It seems we have an unexpected friend."

"Who?" Thresi asked.

Atlas sheathed his blade and started to walk away.

"You'll find out eventually," he replied.

The duo walked out of the camp and entered the forest, where a huge mass of green scales ambushed Thresi.

"Are you all right?" Sparks asked worriedly.

"I'm fine," said Thresi.

"That's good. It's just that everyone else was here and you weren't, so I was worried."

Thresi hugged Sparks and mounted her. Milo got on behind her. Soon, the group was in the night sky, flying toward Edron. From there, they would go to Stomio.

23

Soon Emotions Should Emerge

FOR SEVEN DAYS, the group traveled by night and slept by day. The trip was filled with sleeplessness, irritation, and anything that could make an already bad trip worse. When Milo said they were close to Edron, only Thresi believed him. Even she had her doubts. Things didn't seem good for Milo. He seemed sad, almost in despair. When anyone talked to him, he didn't respond right away. It was like his mind was on something else. Thresi had a feeling that the group couldn't escape trouble's menacing grasp. It seemed to squeeze the life out of them.

On the morning of the seventh day, Milo woke breathing heavily. Thresi woke from her dreams of Stomio to hear Milo softly sobbing to himself.

She quietly walked toward him and asked, "What's wrong?"

Milo went rigid. He didn't hear Thresi coming. He wiped his tears and said, "Nothing's wrong. I'm just thinking."

His voice was shaky, which only proved that Thresi heard him cry.

"Last time I checked, thinking doesn't make you cry. Well, except if you are thinking of something sad," Thresi said jokingly.

Milo smiled at her. They heard something moving behind them. Suddenly, a large, scaly, green head shot in front of them.

"Why are you guys awake?" Sparks asked, "Are we close to Edron?"

Milo shushed Sparks, but it was too late. They heard a groan and some mumbling in Roguish as Atlas came into view.

"Why are you three up?" he asked, stifling a yawn.

Sparks laughed at Atlas as he walked toward them. His hair was sticking up to one side. His tunic was falling off one shoulder, and his vest was only halfway on.

Atlas raised his eyebrow and said, "At least I'm not covered in mud."

Sparks gave him offended look.

Suddenly, mud hit Atlas, and a voice said, "Now you are."

Atlas turned to see Tiger sitting on Zatern, holding her stomach and laughing.

"Ha! Very funny, Tiger," he said, wiping the mud off his face.

Thresi and Milo laughed. Zatern sighed and said, "If you are done with your nonsense, perhaps we can head into the city."

"So we are close to Edron?" Sparks asked excitedly.

Zatern nodded his head.

"Then what are we waiting for? Let's go!" Thresi cheered.

"You guys, go ahead and pack up camp. I need to wake up Katan," Atlas said, fixing his clothes and straightening his hair. He walked toward the sleeping dragon. "Wake up, Katan."

Katan growled and swung his tail, which hit Atlas. The force sent him flying into Milo and knocked him down.

"Sorry about that, Milo," said Atlas.

"I would feel much better if you would get off me," Milo said in a muffled voice.

Atlas stood up, walked toward Katan again, and said, "Katan, either you wake up or you don't get fed."

That got Katan's attention, his black head shot up, and he quickly stood.

"Atlas," he said, wrapping his neck around his rider, "feed me now."

Atlas immediately grabbed whatever was left of their meat and gave it to Katan, who wolfed it done.

"What an entertaining show," Tiger said, trying to suppress laughter. "But we should head into Edron now."

"What about the dragons. Surely the people of Edron haven't seen dragons?" Milo asked.

"You are right, All-Seer, but they have seen Zodiacs before. The people think we are some strange culture of Humans. They believe Zodiacs and Humans can freely trade with each other," Tiger said, still sitting astride Zatern's long neck.

"Is a Zodian boat big enough for the dragons to land on?" Thresi asked.

Atlas laughed and said, "Is a Zodian boat big enough? Ha!"

Tiger shot him a look of annoyance.

"Zodian boats are very large, Thresi," Tiger said, smiling.

Sparks stomped her foot and asked, "Are we leaving or not?"

Tiger laughed and dismounted Zatern.

"Sparks and Katan, follow Zatern to the boat. Await orders from Captain Wolf," Tiger said.

Katan groaned and said, "Not Captain Wolf! What did I do to deserve such torture?"

Atlas laughed as the dragons soon took off into the air.

"Shall we head into the city?" Milo asked nervously.

Everyone nodded their heads and walked toward the city.

The city was huge and filled with so many sights and sounds that it was hard for Thresi to hear her own thoughts. But there was one minor complication. The city was filled with soldiers, undoubtedly because most All-Seers were trying to get Stomio before getting caught and transported. Thresi noticed that Milo seemed really nervous.

"Maybe it's the atmosphere," she thought as she pivoted through the busy streets.

Everything was going fine until Tiger and Atlas stopped.

"Atlas and I are going to go ahead to the ship, just to...you know...check on things," Tiger said nervously.

Atlas looked at her confusedly and said, "We are?"

He winced as Tiger elbowed him in his arm.

"So you're actually going ahead to make sure nothing dangerous is going to get in our way," Milo said in a matter-of-fact tone.

"That about sums it up," Tiger said, dragging Atlas away.

Milo and Thresi just shrugged at each other and slowly followed Tiger's trail.

Something was nagging Thresi, like the sense that something or someone was following them. Her suspicions were soon proven correct when she heard the sound of running footsteps. She suddenly heard Milo yelp in anguish. She turned to see soldiers wrestling Milo to the ground, but these weren't ordinary soldiers like the ones who had captured them in Clot. These soldiers were the king's elite guard trained at being stealthily and quick. Thresi immediately tried to fight off the guards, but they were too quick. One of the guards threw a round ball on the ground, which secreted a thick smoke. Soon, Thresi could no longer see the guards.

"Milo! Milo!" Thresi screamed with tears in her eyes.

She thought she heard Milo yelling in the

distance. She didn't dwell on the sound, but she ran as fast toward the direction that Tiger and Atlas were heading.

When Thresi reached the dock, she saw a huge ship larger than the three dragons combined. Tiger and Atlas were climbing the ramp.

"Tiger! Atlas! Help!" Thresi called.

Tiger and Atlas turned around as Thresi ran into Atlas, sobbing hysterically in his arm.

"What's wrong, Thresi?" Atlas said, rubbing her back soothingly.

Thresi calmed down and said, "The royal guard took Milo. We've got to go after them."

Tiger and Atlas only shook their heads.

"We can't go after them. It would be too dangerous. We can't afford that because we are so close to Stomio," Tiger said sadly.

Thresi started sobbing as they lead her to the boat.

24

Stir in Some Friendship

THRESI FOUND NO comfort during her time at sea. It seemed that everything reminded her that Milo was gone and there was nothing she could do about it. She had met Capitan Wolf, whose gray, tough outside could never hide the fact that he felt sorry for her loss. Another strange character she met was Tiger's older brother, Owl. Thresi noted that Owl and Tiger had a very close relationship, just like the one she and Milo shared. And even though Thresi's birthday was coming up in a week, she could find no happiness in turning thirteen.

When her birthday came, she found no need to celebrate. She had more important things to do. But soon she found herself looking off at the sea on the night of her birthday.

"So this is how Humans celebrate their birthdays. I have always been curious," a voice next to her said.

Thresi kept staring at the sea. In a sad, empty

voice, she said, "Owl, how did you know it was my birthday?"

"For being the birthday girl, you don't seem very happy. When Tiger had her thirteenth birthday, she did nothing but brag. What makes you so different?" asked Owl.

"I'm just not in the mood to celebrate," Thresi answered.

A part of her wanted Owl to leave, but she liked being able to talk to someone.

"Well, it's obvious something is bothering you, but what?" Owl asked, smiling with his golden eyes gleaming.

"You seemed to know it was my birthday. How come you don't know what's bothering me?" asked Thresi.

"Well," Owl replied, "I was hoping you'd tell me own your own. But to answer your question, yes, I do know why you are upset."

Thresi turned and looked at him. Owl's white hair rustled in the sea breeze. His speckled skin gleamed with the moonlight of the three-quarter moon.

She turned back to the ocean and angrily said, "It's my fault he's gone! I should have sensed the soldiers coming. But I got distracted and assumed everything was going to be smooth sailing. But fate just had to prove me wrong!"

Tears brimmed in her eyes, and she thought, "I'm not going to cry."

The only sound to be heard was the sound of the waves lapping at the boat and the quiet whispering of the sailors.

Owl simply put his arm around her and said soothingly, "I've learned from past experiences that not everything that goes wrong is your fault. I remember when my little sister went on her first Guardian mission."

Thresi raised her eyebrow. Owl simply said, "It's when a Guardian travels to one of the other Guardian headquarters. Sort of like what you're doing by going to Stomio."

"Let me guess. Her mission went awry, and you thought it was your fault, but it wasn't because it was Tiger's fault for not paying attention to what she was doing," Thresi replied, making it Owl's turn to raise an eyebrow.

"Now how did you know that?" he asked surprised.

"That's how most brother-sister stories go," she answered confidently.

Owl laughed and said, "You're right. Just remember that what happened to your brother isn't your fault, okay?"

Thresi nodded.

"Then good night and happy birthday," said Owl.

"Good night and thanks," Thresi replied.

Owl smiled and nodded. Thresi watched as Owl walked across the boat and disappeared behind the mast.

Sparks landed next to Thresi and yelled, "Happy birthday, Thresi!"

Thresi couldn't help but smile at Sparks' chipper attitude. Sparks took the news about Milo fairly well after she stopped crying.

"Thank you, Sparks," Thresi said, hugging the dragon's neck. "Can we go flying?"

"Of course!" Sparks answered.

Thresi clambered onto her back, and Sparks took off into the starry sky.

Soon, they were in the sky, soaring through the moonlight.

"It's beautiful," Thresi thought.

The breeze was salty and soothing as it blew Thresi's brown hair behind her. Thresi soon found herself drifting off to sleep.

Epilogue

Serve the Soup in a Bowl

Two weeks passed. The boat soon arrived on Stomio's shore. The crew disembarked the ship, and the cargo was unloaded. Katan immediately went hunting with Atlas, as Tiger flew off to announce their arrival to the Guardian headquarters. But Thresi and Sparks stayed behind and looked across the sea toward Quint.

Thresi stood up straight and said, "I will come back for you, Milo. That's a promise."

She mounted Sparks and flew after Tiger. She, with Sparks at her side, was ready to brave anything that fate threw at her.

Rogue Language

Annatopa: bringer of light
Arsine: the cursed land
Atlas: Earth
Cor-taka siewr: relax a little
Dorande: volcano
Katan: lazy or literally reluctant
Killts ir hu grentics thses Zodian henuens crvebs yitis lt: Perhaps it is possible that Zodian healers could fix it.
Stompina: good morning
Thresi (from Rouge mythology): follow me; the person believed to lead Arsine into light

Zodiac Language

Hinosla, Tiger stri Zatern: Good morning, Tiger and Zatern.
Milo: one who sees all

Stomio: sanctuary for all

Stonti, shalan truistin, mentso natsal de Tiger: Hello, young Guardian. My name is Tiger.

Zatern: the Zodiac god of the moon

Here's an excerpt Rachel Econ's next book

The Devil's Guide to the People Around You

A month later on a Friday after school Aaron, Zeke, and Cali were helping her older brother, Daniel, pick out an apartment.

"This is the last one kids," Daniel said as he parked his mustang near the curb. Zeke and Aaron hopped out of the backseat stretching their legs. Cali stood by one of the windows and peered through the glass.

"It's really dark in there," she said, moving away from the window. Daniel pulled out a key and opened the door.

"Shall we begin our tour?" he asked as they entered the house. Aaron and Zeke shrugged which was the universal sign for Cali to take over.

"Boys", Cali thought, *"can't do a thing for themselves"*. She led them through the kitchen and to the bathroom but when she reached the bedroom she stopped dead in her tracks.

"Guys," she said, voice shaking. "Look." Everyone looked in the room and it was empty except for melting candles, about five pentagrams drawn in blood, and a human skull filled with something black. Daniel pushed the kids away from the room but they stepped back to the door frame and stared.

"What the heck?" Zeke asked.

"That's freaking nasty," Cali said with disgust.

"Weird," Aaron said with a bit of awe in his tone. He looked down and noticed a leather book about the size of a rather large chapter book. He couldn't read the tittle. He started walking toward it when Daniel grabbed him by his collar and pulled him back.

"Don't Aaron," he said angrily as he let go of Aaron's collar. "I don't want you to get hurt."

"By what, man?" Zeke said peering in the room one last time. "Looks like some freaky Goth kids were having their own brand of fun."

Both Cali and Daniel shook their head. Aaron lifted his hands in surrender and said, "Sorry Dan, didn't mean to be curious."

Daniel rolled his eyes and walked toward the front door with Cali following quickly behind. Zeke soon followed. When they turned away from the room Aaron ran into it and picked up the book.

" 'The Devil's Guide to the People Around you'...What the heck?" he asked as he left the room. He quickly shoved the book into his backpack. Female laughter filled the air as it filled Aaron with gnawing fear. He ran to the front door where he nearly collided with Zeke's back.

"Whoa, Aaron what's got you running?" Zeke asked jokingly. Aaron didn't answer but just glanced back at the door. He swore heard female laughter but all was silent. He climbed into the back seat and said nothing the whole way to his house.

Printed in the United States
124048LV00001B/229-246/P